A Lady and A Scholar

Wendy May Andrews

Sparrow Ink
www.sparrowink.com

ISBN - 978-1-989634-84-4

www.wendymayandrews.com

Stay in touch with Wendy May Andrews
and all her upcoming publishing news.

Sign up for her biweekly newsletter at
wendymayandrews.com

Contents

Gaining wealth and independence could cost her everything – including her chance at true love.

After her rich husband's sudden death, Lady Evangeline refuses to remarry for convenience--especially not the handsome but cranky mathematician helping her gain financial independence. Sean Smythe has good reason to hate all things English, especially ones with titles. But when the lovely lady asks for his mathematical help with her economies, he can't help but say yes.

But when Evangeline's in-laws start a fight over her inheritance, they fight dirty, even dragging Sean's history into their scandal. Despite her wish for quiet independence, her sense of justice won't allow her to let Sean fight the battle for her.

As her alliance with Sean grows deeper, Eve is forced to choose between newfound wealth or one last chance at the happiness and love she never realized she craved.

If you're enamored of the manners and pageantry of Jane Austen's Regency, you'll adore this sweet regency romance adventure.

Dedication

In *A Lady and A Scholar*, Eve is trying to find a home for herself where she'll feel safe and welcome. We all need that and I truly wish that for you. I hope you will feel warm and cozy as you enjoy this great read

XO

Acknowledgements

Acknowledgment number one has to go to my truest companion, Mr. Andrews. Thank you for knowing and caring about my Gentlemen nearly as much as I do. My writer's journey has been an adventurous ride. It was much improved by being on it with you. You're the best partner a lady could ask for. Thanks for everything – totally vague but all encompassing.

Acknowledgment number two must go to my parents. Thank you for always supporting me in my endeavors. I love that you have read all of my books, even multiple times. Thanks too for reading to me when I was little – you started me on the road of a love of words.

To my beta readers – Alfred, Monique, Suzanne, and Christina – thank you so much for cheering for my characters, finding the plot holes, and making great suggestions to make my stories better.

I must also take a moment to acknowledge my lost beta reader and the reason why I write in the Regency era. Marlene was one of the most inspiring people I've had the privilege to know. I can't wait to see her again one day soon. Gone for now but never forgotten. My work will always benefit from having been influenced by her.

My gorgeous cover is thanks to the artistry of Andrew at Sparrow Ink.

Thanks to Bev Kaufman and Julie Sherwood for the great edits. Any remaining mistakes are entirely the author's fault.

Chapter One

Lady Evangeline tried to swallow the lump of anxiety in her throat as delicately as possible. She was fairly certain she could trust her maid wouldn't tattle to anyone that she had been so gauche as to gulp, but there was no guarantee there wasn't someone else watching her.

It felt to her as though there was always someone watching. Watching and judging.

The ever-silent Gladys wasn't necessarily one of those judging her. Eve had never grown close to her personal maid, and she didn't completely trust her because she had been hired by Gerald, but despite the woman's quiet watchfulness, Eve suspected there could be warmth in her gaze.

But everyone else watched her with cold assessment. It caused a slither of fear in her spine. It also made her startle at nearly every shadow.

Evangeline suppressed a sigh and almost shook her head in disgust. Now she was becoming paranoid, it would seem. But she had reason considering how much her late husband's family hovered over her.

Having grown up the daughter of an impoverished earl, she had thought her childhood was repressive with all its rules and regulations. That had been nothing compared to the expectations pushed upon her by her bourgeois husband.

Gerald had made Eve feel as though he didn't believe she could think for herself. He certainly hadn't asked for her opinion on anything. He had often told her what he expected her to do. She had followed his directions, making an effort to live up to his expectations. And despite his death, she still felt obliged to continue to do so.

Of course, that obligation was regularly reinforced by the family. Again, Evangeline had to work hard to prevent the sigh threatening to escape her delicate throat. It happened every time she thought about Gerald's family.

She really ought to think of them as her family by now, but she had never been able to do so. Not that they really invited her to do so.

Eve thought of her interaction with Ralph the night before.

"Mrs. Robertson tells me you haven't been accepting many of the invitations that come for you. Is there a reason for your reticence?"

"A reason beyond the fact that I am mourning your brother, do you mean?" Evangeline had asked as gently as she could muster, wondering what the man could possibly have against her remaining at home.

She didn't think he would be able to explain himself but rather than do so, he asked another question. "How else are you to find another husband if you don't go about amongst your people?"

Eve lowered her head and shook it slightly. "It would be a challenge to ever replace Gerald, don't you think?"

"No one said anything about replacing him, my lady," he said heavily. "But at your age, you ought to be thinking about remarriage."

Eve managed to smile gently, nod her head slightly, and leave the room without committing herself to anything nor insulting her brother-in-law.

But now she was more determined than ever to see this errand through. She had managed to get herself out of the house that morning without anyone stopping her. Now she needed to carry on.

Eve didn't even bother trying to suppress her sigh now, but she covered it over with movement. Forward movement. The kind that entailed climbing down from the carriage she was sitting in.

Her patience was at an end, both with her restless thoughts and with waiting for a servant to appear. No footman had yet arrived to open the door for her. This led her to believe that the rumours circulating about the unconventional household were true.

That was reassuring. It was part of why she had come. And she was surely capable of opening a carriage door for herself. There was nothing to be concerned about. The family need never know. And even if they did, there couldn't possibly be anything to question in her visiting the former Miss Lucy Scranton, now Mrs. Northcott, the daughter-in-law of the Earl of Everleigh and the sister of Viscount Scranton.

No one in their right mind would consider a connection of the earl to be bad *ton*. And the viscount and his lovely wife were accepted everywhere. Really, it could be argued, Eve was doing her duty to the family by making such a call.

That wasn't, of course, to say that the family were in their right mind, so it was very possible they would consider the visit highly questionable. Knowing them as she now did, Eve wouldn't be surprised if they were to take exception to her visit to the unconventional place. They expected her to be everything that was completely conventional. Too bad that didn't really interest her any longer.

It had used to. If one were to ask her, although who really would, she would have answered absolutely, she was the most conventional of ladies. But she didn't actually consider herself conventional now that she was considering the matter. For one thing, she had no desire to remarry.

According to absolutely everyone in her life, she ought to be pursuing remarriage at the earliest opportunity, now that she was out of the prescribed full mourning. She wasn't getting any younger, for one thing.

It struck Evangeline as perfectly odd that Gerald's family thought she ought to marry. From what she understood of their thinking, she would have thought they would have expected her to have burned herself on a pyre as she knew was expected of widows in some foreign lands.

That just went to prove that she didn't understand the family in the least. Because they had made it very clear to her that she ought to marry a nobleman. Somehow, in their convoluted reasoning, this would elevate them even further in Society than Gerald's marriage to her had done.

And Evangeline now fully understood that was, in their estimation, her purpose in life. Through their association with her, they expected to become accepted into High Society.

It was the dreariest concept Eve could imagine.

She didn't know how to explain to them that absolutely nothing would make them acceptable to the *ton*. Certainly not their association with a mere daughter of an earl. Especially not one who had been forced to marry money.

She didn't even have a title in her own right, merely a courtesy title due to being her father's daughter. And theirs wasn't even that old a title. Eve's brother was only the fourth earl. Hardly anything to crow about.

But crow the family did. Which only went to prove her point. How could they not know that true nobility didn't have to announce themselves?

All these thoughts were chasing themselves through her mind even as she admonished herself for dithering. There was no reason to be nervous.

She was perfectly within her rights to make a call on a friend, even if said friend was less than conventional. And she was almost certain she could trust her maid. What she was less sure of was whether or not the family had set watchers other than her personal servant upon her.

But watchers couldn't be here at the Alldred place. They were isolated enough that anyone following her would have to be unmistakeably visible, especially when one considered there weren't enough trees along the drive to be able to successfully hide. On the other hand, though, there wasn't much out this way, so if she were seen coming in this direction, it could safely be assumed this was her destination.

Perhaps she had finally lost her mind.

Evangeline forced herself out of her inertia with a determination that was unusual for her. She was a lady, she reminded herself. An adult lady at that. She had the ability to decide for herself how she would spend her day. It wasn't up to her dead husband's family to dictate her behavior.

If only that were true, she thought with another sigh as she heard the rustle of her maid climbing out of the carriage behind her. It didn't take hearing the servant's sniff to know the other woman disapproved of their lack of reception. Eve could feel the skepticism rolling off the servant like the waves of the sea.

It was for that reason Evangeline didn't even glance behind herself. She was not to be deterred. The maid could follow or not, that was up to her, but Eve was moving forward.

She had hesitated long enough. She was here. It would be even more ridiculous if she had come all this way and didn't knock.

It would be an admission that she shouldn't have come. That would never do.

A quick glance around showed the property was well cared for. And it was quite extensive. One could argue it was a prosperous estate. The family was likely to think so if they were to hear a report of it.

They might think the residents weren't sufficiently fashionable for her to bother with, but it couldn't be argued that they were unacceptable. Evangeline was counting on that fact.

With a nod and a further stiffening of her backbone, Lady Evangeline walked toward Mrs. Northcott's front door as though she were entering the ballroom of the highest *ton*. Because really, any connection of Everleigh was the highest *ton*. No one could argue otherwise, not even the family.

They would likely try, though.

Before she had time to fret over that last thought, even before she could lift the knocker, the door was wrenched open.

"Good afternoon, my lady," a formal servant said after glancing at the mark on the door of the carriage.

His formality was quite at odds with the delay in arriving to welcome her. Evie wondered if he had perhaps come from one of the occupants' former homes. It was an amusing speculation but was neither here nor there as he continued speaking.

"Do come in and tell me who you might like to visit."

Evangeline blinked at the man. Who could he think she was calling upon? Were there any other women in residence besides Mrs. Northcott?

A frown started to form on her forehead, but she quickly nipped that in the bud. A pleasant smile quickly replaced it. She relaxed her shoulders and glanced around the foyer of the larger than expected house, admiring the gleam of the woodwork.

Light filled the area from the large windows flanking the door. Clearly the homeowners weren't concerned about the tax. And however lax the butler or footman might have been about welcoming her, it was obvious any household servants were kept busy about the place. There wasn't even a fleck of dust floating on the air.

"Is Mrs. Northcott at home to visitors?" she asked with a slight nod. It wouldn't do to curtsy to the servant but his bearing almost made her do so.

"I will ascertain. If you would be so good as to take a seat in the salon, a maid will see to bringing you some refreshments."

Amusement threatened to twitch Eve's lips, but she managed to nod once more nearly as regally as the butler before settling herself on the indicated settee. Her own maid nodded in approval as she stared around the comfortable room, much to Eve's surprise. Her maid seemed to think along the same lines as the family. The more formal the better, in their minds.

Eve supposed the butler's formality made up for the informality of the reception room in the servant's mind. It didn't make much difference to Eve. She was just glad she hadn't been turned away before even stepping foot across the threshold.

It wasn't that she wanted to court scandal. She certainly did *not* wish to do so. But she needed help, and she couldn't think of anywhere else to turn for it.

Evangeline didn't have friends or family she could turn to. Her brother would just make her come home if she let on to him that she was unhappy in her current situation. Even if she were willing to return to her childhood home, which she most definitely was not, her brother's solution would be nearly identical to what the family wanted of her.

Marriage to a nobleman. The more noble the better.

Or she could be the aunt in his household, an unpaid companion to his wife and children. Arguably that held even less attraction for her as the prospect of another marriage. No, what she needed was a little help to arrange her affairs. Surely that shouldn't be too much to ask.

Again, a sigh threatened. Eve closed her eyelids for the briefest moment, hardly more than a blink, but it prevented her rolling her eyes at her own silliness. Sighs were useless and not to be borne.

She had allowed herself to get into this mess. She would get herself out of it. She couldn't possibly be as stupid in reality as she had seemed to be in the past. Not anymore. There had to be something good to come out of her experiences.

She had been threatened with the title of bluestocking most of her life. Couldn't all of that reading be of benefit to her for once? Evangeline was determined to prove she wasn't a simpleton. She would find a solution to her dilemma, even if she had to ask for help to do so.

"Oh, I beg your pardon."

The deep male voice sent an almost delicious shiver down her back. *Almost* because Evangeline never enjoyed anything new. She couldn't possibly trust such a delightful sensation. Therefore, it must not be something to enjoy. But she knew if she were a different sort of person, or one with completely different circumstances, it was very likely she would have enjoyed the sensation very much.

Despite her convoluted thoughts, Evangeline turned her attention to the gentleman who was still hovering near the door. The handsome, but slightly absent-minded-looking man was the true reason she had made the drive out to the former Alldred estate. She would never be induced to admit to that fact though.

At her raised eyebrows he stammered out, "I thought Lucy would be here."

"I am waiting for Mrs. Northcott, myself. I believe the butler has gone to see if she is accepting visitors."

Evangeline fought against finding the man's indecision endearing as he hovered in the doorway. She was used to particularly decisive men. But somehow his dithering set her at ease, not a sensation she was familiar with.

She wondered if she ought to invite him to enter or send him on his way. Considering it was in fact him she wanted to meet with, it would be foolish to get rid of him.

But she had no intention of admitting to that just yet.

Chapter Two

Sean Smythe stared at the beautiful young woman and wished he could bolt from the room.

He was pretty sure Roddie would think that unforgivably rude, though, and Sean had no intention of ever offending his best friend and benefactor or the man's lovely wife.

Where was Lucy, by the by? She ought to be here to save him from this predicament.

What was one supposed to say to a woman? A beautiful woman, at that?

If she were a mathematical equation, it would be as easy as pie. Or *pi*, he thought with a smirk.

He shouldn't have done that. He could see immediately that the exotic creature thought his smirk was at her. He wouldn't have thought it possible for her to become any stiffer than she had been when he first stammered his way into the room.

Was he offending her by his mere presence? Was it because there was no chaperone? But didn't the maid count?

Sean ran through all the possibilities in his mind, but he was still undecided. She was stunningly beautiful but appeared as approachable as the frozen pond he had skated upon as a boy.

"You are Mr. Smythe, aren't you?" the beautiful creature asked, making his eyes widen in shock.

"I am, but how could you possibly know that?"

"We have been introduced," she replied calmly.

Sean was certain there was a faint crinkle in the sides of her eyes as though she were considering being amused at him. He didn't mind.

Amusement was his second favorite thing in the world, next to scientific discovery. Perhaps it was because scientific discovery usually brought him vast amounts of amusement. His mind wanted to trail off, but he managed to refocus his attention upon the woman before him.

"My apologies," he finally stammered out with a bow. "I am not usually the forgetful sort."

But then as though the spark of light from one of his inventions illuminated his brain, he remembered Roderick and Lucy's wedding and the ladies the bride had invited. The scholars had all agreed their hostess was trying her hand at matchmaking, but none of them had managed to be entrapped in her endeavour.

Sean brought his attention to account once more and offered the woman another bow.

"My apologies again, my lady, you are quite correct, we have been introduced. And it hasn't even been that long since, has it? How do you do?"

He was still torn between fleeing the scene and performing the social niceties. With a sigh, he stepped further into the room.

Especially knowing who she was, he was certain the Northcotts would expect him to be polite. His sigh must have been louder than he meant it to be. Lady Evangeline's lips finally twitched, but he wasn't sure if it was with an effort to suppress laughter or displeasure.

"I don't wish to interrupt your work, Mr. Smythe. You needn't feel obliged to play nursemaid. I am certain the butler or Mrs. Northcott will be along shortly."

"Stubbs is exceedingly proper, so you are likely right," Sean agreed even as he perched himself carefully on one of the less comfortable chairs in the salon. "Have you just driven out today?" he asked.

Now the lady's smile appeared and it even seemed genuine. "Yes, it was a lovely day for a drive."

"But it's rather far, isn't it?"

The lady inclined her head in agreement before dismissing the concern. "My residence is on the right side of Town for the visit. We didn't have to brave the traffic to get here. And an early start got us here in good time."

"It was a risk, though, to come unannounced, wasn't it?"

Sean knew he shouldn't question the lady in such a forward manner, but his constant need to inquire couldn't be squelched despite his nerves around such a beautiful female. He always needed to know how things worked. There was no way to take apart a human except with questions.

"I do hope it will be worth the risk. Not a very large risk. The horses were happy for the exercise, and I had nothing else planned for the day. If it had rained, that would have made it a chore, but otherwise, even if no one is receiving today, it shan't have been a great loss."

"You must have a particular desire to speak with Lucy, in that case," Sean said the obvious rather lamely.

Her polite but cool smile told Sean that she agreed with his own assessment. Before he could further demonstrate his foolishness, he was saved by the entrance of Lucy Northcott. She bustled into the room in a flurry of motion, her skirts aflutter and with footmen in tow.

"What a delightful surprise, my lady."

Lucy was very welcoming, taking her guest's hand in her own, even dipping into a brief curtsy. Sean blinked in surprise as his eyebrows rose toward his hairline. He thought of Lucy as the highest level of Society but he supposed, since she didn't even have a title, her guest was higher *ton* than she was.

He had to stifle the grin that threatened to spread across his face as he recollected how very foolish the English nobility was. The reasonable part of his brain, though, reminded him that the Scots weren't much better.

Bestowing titles by reason of birth rather than merit was ridiculous whether the titleholders were Scottish or English. He turned his attention back to the room.

"Thank you for seeing me, Mrs. Northcott," Lady Evangeline was saying even as Lucy waved away her words.

"Please, we already agreed we are to be friends, so you must call me Lucy. We don't stand on ceremony in this household."

Sean wondered why the lady's gaze nervously flickered toward her maid at Lucy's remark but then chastised himself for the thought. The lovely woman's face was perfectly serene.

There was nothing to indicate that she was nervous about anything. Perhaps she merely wondered if she ought to dismiss the servant. Or put her to work.

Then Sean worried he ought to leave the room. Not that he wanted to be in the room. Well, he didn't mind gazing upon the beautiful specimen that was Lady Evangeline, but he needn't remain for the conversation if they were going to be engaging in Society gossip. Sean was almost certain Lucy would love to get caught up on the real news from Town.

Not that Lady Evangeline was necessarily fully up to date, he reminded himself. He himself chose to ignore Society gossip for the most part, but he remembered hearing that Lady Evangeline wasn't terribly important socially.

She was a widow now but had been married to a wealthy *cit* from what he could recall. That would make her both envied and reviled, he was sure, just to demonstrate the contrariness of High Society. He really ought to leave the room or his disdain was sure to become evident.

But the conversation had flowed around him while he had been thinking his distracted thoughts and now it was likely too late. Roderick was stepping into the room and clapped him on the shoulder before bowing in greeting to their guest. Sean accepted the inevitable.

Since he had already gotten to his feet when Lucy had entered, he took the opportunity to move further into the room, heading for the chair he considered the least flimsy of his hostess' furnishings.

"What a pleasure to see you, my lady," Roderick Northcott welcomed warmly even as his eyes lingered upon his wife.

Sean could never tire of seeing how much his friend loved his wife. It was supposed to have been a marriage of convenience. Roderick had intentionally set out to marry a well-dowered female so he could establish the Foundation for Scholarly Pursuits. The very foundation that was now sponsoring Sean's studies.

With a start Sean remembered that Lady Evangeline was one of the potential wealthy brides Roderick had considered. Not that Roderick had truly pursued the woman, but she was certainly on his list of possibilities before he settled upon Miss Lucy Scranton.

No one would have ever expected that friendly, gossipy debutante to take so well to being the matron of a society of scholars. But there you had it; they were all rubbing along nicely together with Mrs. Northcott acting as honorary mother or big sister to all the absent-minded scientists in her care.

Never mind that she was the youngest person in residence, Sean thought with a grin as he followed Roderick's example, sitting down and accepting a cup of tea.

Apparently, he wasn't to be leaving the room just yet.

"I was hoping you would accept my invitation to come for a visit," Lucy was exclaiming with delight, even as she turned it into a scold. "But I had wished you would give me some warning and come for a stay, not just a call."

"That is too kind of you, Mrs. Northcott," the lady responded before stumbling at Lucy's obviously censorious expression. "That is to say, Lucy," Lady Evangeline concluded with a slight, nervous giggle, that she quickly cut off as though it hadn't existed.

"It's not too kind, my lady," Lucy countered. "As you no doubt know, this is a male dominated household. I would dearly love to have some feminine company for longer than a cup of tea."

Being the keen observer that he was, Sean couldn't help taking careful note of their visitor's reaction to Lucy's words. It appeared to Sean as though the lady felt struck by Lucy's words. Almost like they had injured her in some way, but Sean couldn't fathom why. Lucy's words hadn't been truly censorious. She was merely complaining that the lady hadn't allowed her to extend further hospitality.

"Perhaps next time?" Lucy said.

Sean wondered if she had realized she had hurt the lady. Lucy was a dear, but she wasn't always quick to notice if others felt differently than she did on matters. She wasn't a scientist after all. Nor was she insecure about anything as far as Sean could tell. She was the strongest, most confident woman he'd ever met, except for maybe his own dear mother.

Sean continued to remain silent and observe the flow of conversation around him. He knew Roddie would expect him to participate. He was considered gentry, after all, due to his father's being a wretched English viscount, or rather those who overlooked the irregularity of his parents' situation considered him such.

In either case, Roddie expected him to act according to Society's norms when Society came to call. But Sean was Scottish at heart, if he had to pick a nation, and a scientist first and foremost. The oddities of the London High Society did not sit well with him, and he struggled to conform to their expectations. Particularly if someone were acting oddly.

And their visitor was certainly doing that.

Sean was torn between observing her and returning to his shed to continue his own studies. Lucy didn't like it when he called his small building a shed. But that is what it had been when Roderick bought his property. Yes, it had now been converted into the perfect workspace for a gentleman who was studying mathematics.

The light was excellent, there were enough shelves for all his quickly accumulating textbooks, large swathes of blackboard for him to work out any tricky problems, and even some table space if he did want to engage in some small experimentation.

Since he had left engineering behind, he didn't need an overlarge space for machinery and construction. But it still used to be a shed. A woodshed if he could recall correctly from his very first visit to the property. He wasn't disparaging it to call it that, in his mind. But to Lucy, he was. So he tried very hard not to say it out loud.

He loved his shed. He loved to spend time in his shed. But he couldn't call it a laboratory as she wished him to.

For one thing, he wasn't mixing any chemicals there. Surely that was what one would do in a laboratory. For another, it was rather pretentious to call a small building for a mathematician a laboratory. Perhaps he could manage if he set his mind to it to call it a library or a salon or even mayhap an office, but not a laboratory.

Lucy Scranton Northcott was brilliant in many ways. But she had some strange notions that he and the others did their best to overlook, considering how kind she and her husband were being to them.

One of the things he had to overlook was her overblown sense of what they were going to accomplish with their studies. She fully expected them all to change the world.

He just wanted to study maths.

And people.

And maybe a little bit of machinery.

Really, why did he have to choose?

Sean was aware there were only twenty-four hours in every day. Well, twenty-four and an eighth, to be precise. And mathematicians required precision. But he wished there were more years expected in his life. There was just so much to learn and observe and study. He hated that he had to pick a specialty.

His loud sigh drew all eyes in the room to him.

"My sincerest apologies," he stammered out as he felt as though a burner had been ignited behind his cheekbones.

Lucy frowned, Evangeline smiled slightly, but Roderick laughed. "Are we boring you, old chap?" he asked with a hearty slap on his shoulder. "Your mind is still on your science, isn't it?"

It was so close to the truth that Sean was embarrassed even further. How rude of him. His mother would have words for him were she to ever learn of it.

But since she was in Edinburgh and he was here, it wasn't likely that she would ever hear of his rudeness. He dismissed the irrelevant thought. It was still exceptionally rude to be caught sighing in company.

Delectable company.

He ought to be applying his mental faculties to why the lady might have called. Their scholarly foundation wasn't exactly right around the corner from Mayfair.

"I do apologize for interrupting your studies, all of you. I suppose I ought to have sent a note that I was coming, but the opportunity was rather an impulse, so I jumped at it."

Sean frowned over the lady's words, wondering if there were a hidden meaning. Did she mean she had decided impulsively? Or that an opportunity had arisen suddenly? Was she not a widow, free to do as she wished? His curiosity was piqued. Lady Evangeline would be his field of study for the time of her visit.

"Absolutely no apology required," Lucy insisted as she topped up everyone's tea. "You'll just have to return another time for a longer visit."

Sean again smiled slightly as the lady murmured something not quite intelligible, as though she weren't accepting or rejecting the invitation. That was a special skill. He ought to learn it.

A few more minutes of pleasantries passed before Sean was surprised by Lucy's next words.

"Would your maid like to have a visit in the kitchens? I didn't think to ask right away."

The way she said it made it sound perfectly reasonable, but Sean wasn't sure if it was usual or not. He suspected a lady's maid might not wish to lower herself to the scullery, but he wasn't certain. Then again, despite her amazing ability to maintain a serene expression, there did appear to be a lightening about her features as Lady Evangeline nodded to her servant, who stood and left the room.

After a moment of silence, Evangeline smiled at Lucy and thanked her.

Lucy waved away the gratitude. “She’s likely to be more comfortable there, and I have a feeling we will be too.”

Sean only noticed it because of his close perusal, but Evangeline appeared shocked by Lucy’s observation. He was further surprised by Lucy’s next words.

“Would you like me to dismiss the gentlemen as well or ought they to hear what you have to say?”

Sean was used to Lucy’s take-charge ways, but it was obvious their guest was not. Her mouth opened and closed, but no words came out for a moment of stunned silence. Then the beautiful lady’s eyes landed on him and he was shocked even further.

Chapter Three

Evangeline thought she might expire from humiliation, but she should have expected the intelligent people of the Scholarly Society to see right through her attempts at hiding her truth. She had faced embarrassment many times before and had not died from it, but somehow this time felt worse.

It had been foolishness on her part to think they wouldn't be able to tell she was hiding something. They were scientists after all.

Besides, there was no need to hide the truth from these ones. How was she to gain their assistance without confiding in them? And at least Mrs. Northcott had the discretion to dismiss the servants before putting her on the spot.

It was perfectly acceptable, natural even, to send the servants to visit in the kitchens. Wasn't it? That wouldn't alert the family to her purpose in visiting the unconventional household, would it?

Evangeline needed to stop procrastinating. She had come for a reason. She needed to address it and then be on her way. If she hoped to convince the family it had been a mere social call, she couldn't linger overlong.

She turned her focus to Mr. Smythe and finally answered Mrs. Northcott's offer to dismiss him from the room.

"I actually called to ask for Mr. Smythe's assistance, so I do hope he would stay and hear me out."

Evangeline could see she had shocked them all. Well, that was just as well. Turn about was fair play, wasn't it? She had been shocked by her hostess' perception, thinking she had hidden her intentions so well.

"But of course, we are all at your disposal, my lady. Tell us how we might be of help," Mrs. Northcott answered immediately while her husband nodded and Mr. Smythe merely appeared dumfounded.

After a moment of silence wherein Evangeline was unsure how to proceed after the scientist appeared so shocked, Mrs. Northcott prompted her.

"Are you in some sort of trouble, my lady? How can we help you? And what does Sean have to do with it?"

Heat flooded her cheeks as though a fire had been lit nearby, but Evangeline forced herself to continue ignoring her embarrassment. It was worse to leave her hosts with questions after declaring she needed assistance, she was certain. Not that she had ever heard of such a situation.

Was there even a proper social protocol for such a case?

Eve knew she was dithering. She cleared her throat as delicately as she could in order to rid herself of the tightness there and finally began speaking. After glancing at Mr. Smythe, Eve kept her gaze on Mrs. Northcott but gestured toward the scientist as she spoke.

"We met at your wedding, of course. But I actually saw him at an event a few weeks ago and while we didn't exchange conversation, I overheard him briefly telling someone about his new field of study. Previously I had understood Mr. Smythe's interests lay in the engineering field, but he explained to his associate that he had shifted his focus to studying economics and the maths involved with how economies function."

"A gentleman should be able to pursue more than one field of study, shouldn't he?" Mr. Smythe interjected, sounding sulky.

Evangeline wasn't sure how to respond to the distraction, nor was it relevant to her purposes, so she ignored it for the time being.

"I could use his advice on matters of economics. And perhaps some legal matters might need advising on, as well. I don't suppose you have an expert in the law hanging about the place?" she asked with a light laugh that sounded a little forced to her ears but resulted in warm smiles from the Northcott couple.

"No lawyers on retainer here, but Roderick is well versed in most matters and will be happy to help you in any way he can."

Evangeline had to laugh at the expression on the gentleman's face at his wife's words. He appeared torn between agreeing with her and wishing to argue with her.

Eve surmised that in theory he agreed but didn't appreciate being told what he was going to do by his slip of a wife. If she were going to be spending any amount of time with the pair, Eve knew it was going to be highly diverting to witness their interaction.

"Is it a matter that can be resolved very quickly, do you suppose?" Mrs. Northcott asked when it didn't appear Evangeline was going to add any more information.

Eve sighed a little before she cut the sound short. "That is doubtful, unfortunately."

Mrs. Northcott gave her a decisive nod.

"It is as I thought, you ought to have come for a stay, not just a call."

She sounded as though she were going to scold further but then she clapped her hands together and urged Evangeline, "Tell us what you can now and we will make a start, then we will set a time where you can come for an extended stay. Should you leave your maid at home?"

Surprised by the young matron's perception and wishing she could agree, Evangeline shook her head. "That would cause more problems than it would solve."

Mrs. Northcott nodded firmly again. "Very well. Should you return in a se'en-night? Or is it more urgent than that?"

This time Evangeline couldn't stop her sigh.

"It isn't truly urgent at all," she admitted before blurting out the rest. "I just don't care to continue as the matters stand now. I want to see if I can set up an independent household for myself, you see."

The other occupants of the room had varying degrees of frowns upon their face. It would have been amusing if she weren't so very concerned about her own situation.

"I would have thought you were considered independent already. Is your husband not dead, after all?"

Mr. Northcott appeared as though he were trying to ask delicately, but how does one ask such a thing?

Evangeline actually laughed slightly.

"Oh, no, he is well and truly dead. I checked. But his family has taken it upon themselves to carry on his style of running the household. I would like to have one of my own, but I'm not sure if I can. They will resist, for certain. But legally and economically I have come to ask for your assistance in determining if it is possible."

Mrs. Northcott clapped her hands in what appeared to be delight this time. "How perfectly practical. We will all of us delight in helping you with this. Thank you for coming to us. I have been wishing we could do something to assist you."

Evangeline blinked and stared. "How could you have known that I was in need of assistance?"

The usually self-assured young matron blushed and her eyes flickered toward her husband with a slight frown creasing her forehead, seemingly in consternation.

"I didn't, exactly, I was just hoping we could do a good turn for you."

Trying not to frown in return, Eve's glance flickered between the faces of each occupant of the room. Both Northcotts appeared embarrassed but determined to ride it out. Mr. Smythe finally laughed and offered an explanation of sorts as he looked at Roderick Northcott.

"She was on your list, wasn't she?"

Mr. Northcott's frown was fierce and Evangeline suspected if there weren't women present, fisticuffs would have erupted from the gentlemen.

"One doesn't talk of such things in company," Mr. Northcott said firmly even as his wife giggled and added, "One shouldn't talk of such things at all."

Mrs. Northcott turned to Evangeline and offered an explanation.

"I do apologize, Lady Evangeline, our household isn't always as strict with certain niceties as we ought to be. We are often distracted by our scientific pursuits."

Again, the woman's gaze flickered to meet that of her husband.

"But Sean wasn't wrong in his statement. I have wanted to do you a service, since I have felt as though I stole a march on you with Roderick."

"I beg your pardon," was all Evangeline could think to say as heat engulfed her. "I swear to you, Mrs. Northcott, there was never anything between your husband and me."

"Oh, I realize that. But it was a possibility once. And it would have benefited you immensely, I'm sure," she added with a flirtatious glance at her husband. "So I feel as though I did you a disservice and would like to compensate you in some way."

Evangeline wondered if she had accidentally stumbled into a madhouse. Laughter threatened to overtake her despite her previous embarrassment and she mentally shrugged.

She didn't really care what misguided notion led to the strange people helping her. If they offered her the assistance she needed, she would be both pleased and relieved, whatever their strange reasoning behind it.

Still fighting to contain her amusement so as to not offend her hosts, Evangeline inclined her head in acknowledgement, especially when it finally dawned on her what the other woman meant.

"That rout, last Season. It seemed as though Mr. Northcott was far more social than usual. Is that what you are referring to?"

Evangeline wanted to giggle when the others all shifted guiltily.

"I would appreciate your help with my dilemma, but I cannot allow you to foster a guilty conscience over the matter. Everyone who has seen you will agree you appear uncommonly suited for one another, and I have no intention of remarrying, so you wouldn't have had much success had you thought to pursue a courtship with me."

"But I thought you were looking for a husband," Mrs. Northcott blurted out.

"That is what the gossips would have you believe. And the family, of course. They don't much care if anyone believes it, though. That is their intention. That I marry. The higher along the social scale the better, in their opinion. Which is why I have come to you."

Now everyone appeared confused, and Evangeline couldn't contain her amusement any longer. She allowed herself to laugh for a brief moment, a true laugh, and then sobered.

"I do apologize. I am evidently making a complete mull of this. But I didn't expect certain turns of events. But never mind that. I haven't come for matchmaking, I promise you. I would like your help in ensuring my independence."

"Ah, yes, the legalities and the economics. That makes much more sense now."

Mrs. Northcott appeared relieved to better understand.

"It doesn't matter what the reasons are, we will be delighted to help in any way we can."

She then turned to Mr. Smythe as though to twit him. "See, Sean, your change of focus will be rewarded almost immediately."

"Happy to help," the gentleman replied with a bashful bow.

"Now that the awkwardness is out of the way," Mrs. Northcott said with a delicate wave of her hand and a light laugh, "do you want to tell us the details now or work out when you can come back for a stay and to really delve into the matter?"

Evangeline was a little taken aback. She had spent all her time hoping they would help her but hadn't really given much thought to what she would do once they had agreed. She had thought the matter through over and over at great length, though. She was ready to discuss it now.

"It would probably be best to tell you what my issue is first, and then you can give it some thought in the meantime. That way it might be easier to resolve when I return."

"Smart lady," Mr. Smythe remarked, clearly thinking out loud.

Evangeline smiled shyly. "Thank you, Mr. Smythe."

"I rather suspect we can dispense with all the formalities if we're going to be discussing your personal matters, don't you?" Mr. Northcott, or rather Roderick, pointed out.

"Thank you. And you all must call me Evangeline or even just Eve."

"Very well, so, Eve, do tell us what you would like to accomplish. I would have expected a widow such as yourself would have no real need for economies."

Roderick Northcott was looking at her as though he were wondering if he ought to curtail her shopping or slay her dragons. Evangeline almost burst into inappropriate giggles once more.

"To be completely frank, I am not certain what my affairs might be. I have been prevented from speaking with the solicitor on various occasions for the most nonsensical reasons. I suspect my husband's family might be afraid of being cut off from his wealth. But they also wish for me to wed once more. They are a most confusing lot. I am nearly certain they mean well in some strange way, but I have no desire to pander to their wishes on either front. If they aren't meant to be forever sitting on my financial skirts, then I don't see why I must put up with their control over my life."

She bit her lip and looked out the window into the gardens in an effort to control her emotions. She could see that it was a lovely estate the Northcotts had settled into. It seemed perfectly suited to their eclectic taste and needs. She tried not to sigh with despair or jealousy. Eve turned back to Lucy with her thoughts and feelings somewhat more controlled.

"You must have suspected something, else you wouldn't have sent my maid away."

"Oh, it's not so strange to send the servants to the kitchens. Doesn't that happen when you make your calls?"

Evangeline's smile felt tight.

"I haven't a great deal of experience, to be honest. I didn't have a proper debut, as my father had already run through all his money, including my dowry."

"Never say so," Roderick objected, clearly shocked at the thought that a father could do such a thing.

He appeared embarrassed to have said so out loud, though.

"My apologies for interrupting," he added.

Rather than being put out, Evangeline was touched by his reaction, but she didn't want to speak ill of her late father.

"I think Father must have suffered from addictions of some sort. There doesn't seem to be another explanation, unless he were perhaps somehow unhinged."

She shrugged as though to dismiss the topic.

"He found my Gerald. It could have been far worse. The man meant to be a kind-hearted husband. And he never beat me."

Lucy made a soft sound of distress. "Those are not rousing endorsements, I'm sorry to say."

Evangeline's smile was a little forced. "Perhaps not, but my father and brother benefited. And I'm happy to report that my brother seems to be much better equipped to bring the estate about than my father ever had been."

"I've heard of some of his modernizations," Sean added. "He has some intriguing ideas. Lincoln, one of the other fellows, plans to call upon him."

"Oh, I'm sure he would be most welcome to share any ideas he might have. My brother has gone quite mad trying to develop his herds and crops and such.

But it is keeping them fed and even turning a profit, so I cannot despise his ideas."

Sean's frown turned fierce. Evangeline wished she could know what he was thinking. But reading people had never been her forte.

Chapter Four

Sean was swept with a sudden and uncharacteristic desire to slay dragons and burn bridges. It was an unusual sensation to be sure.

A part of him wished he could examine the feelings further, ascertaining the source and what it might mean. But even he, in all his distracted innocence, knew it would be unacceptable to depart from the conversation in order to better understand why he wanted to protect a woman.

On the surface, it wasn't that difficult to understand. Lady Evangeline was beautiful in an understated way. It was as though she were trying to hide her beauty. Sean might not be overly experienced in Society matters, but even he knew ladies never tried to minimize their attractions.

On the contrary, most wanted to boost them or even exaggerate them.

He blinked his eyes and tried not to frown at her. His first assessment was correct, though. Even though he didn't understand anything about women's fashions, he could tell from looking at her that Lady Evangeline wasn't trying to enhance her beauty.

Her hair was scraped back far tighter than he thought was fashionable. While Lucy had curls artfully springing about her head in little clumps that were quite fetching, her ladyship's hair seemed to be reined in as though she couldn't bear for a single strand to go unconstrained.

And while it was likely impossible to hide her femininity, Sean suspected she had chosen the heavy fabric and drab colour of her gown to make the attempt. Of course, she wasn't long out of her mourning period, she might have loved her husband and was trying to honour his memory.

But he realized his impulse to protect the lady actually lay in her inner beauty. The strength and resilience she displayed, also in an understated manner. It was as though she were accustomed to hiding her true self in all matters.

It was both intriguing and irritating. Why would a well born woman hide who she really was?

Sean's scientific impulses were intrigued in addition to his manly desire to protect a lovely woman. Too bad she was so very English, he thought with a grimace he hoped no one noticed. If not for that unavoidable fact, it wouldn't be much of a chore to spend time with her, whatever the problem might be.

From his recollection, Sean was certain he had never met the lady's now-deceased husband, but from the gossip he had heard, the man had been exceedingly wealthy. There was no reasonable explanation for her thinking she might not have the funds to set herself up. Surely she had been well provided for, even if the man had other heirs he had left the bulk of his estate to.

So why was she there asking for help? Why really?

Surely there would be a barrage of solicitors and bankers more than willing to answer any questions she might have about her settlements. Surely there were settlements, he thought with a sudden lurch. Or perhaps the woman had been left destitute.

It wasn't completely unheard of, despite how despicable it sounded to Sean. He spared a thought for his much-loved mother and how she had been left. That thought reminded him that he couldn't believe he was in England. His stomach turned.

Why was he in this room, considering helping the beautiful daughter of an English earl? Surely no one would expect it of him. Not truly.

But then, Roderick had never actually believed that Sean hated the English quite as fiercely as he truly did. And Roderick had earned Sean's loyalty through his own.

Sean was torn.

If Roderick asked him to help this woman, he would have to do it, despite her being English gentry. It wouldn't be a betrayal of his mother as long as the woman was no relation to Sean's father. If she were, he would have to decline Roderick and Lucy's offer of his help no matter what that might do to his relationship with them. In fact, if they would insist upon it, perhaps he wouldn't really wish to have a relationship with them in any case.

That would be a massive sacrifice, of course. But one had to stick to their ideals. Otherwise, you were nothing but an animal. An animal like his father. And like the man's other sons likely were.

But that wasn't an issue he ought to be thinking about in Lucy's receiving room. Despite her being an English gentlewoman, Sean had liked her quite well from the very beginning of their acquaintance

Roderick would have his head for thinking of his relationship with Lucy as mere acquaintance. But it was hard for him to truly consider anyone English to be a friend. Roderick was the main exception. As his wife, Sean supposed Lucy could be considered part of that package.

With a nod, Sean accepted that Lucy was his friend. And then he firmly turned his attention to the problem facing a friend of his friends. Or at least the acquaintance of his friends.

Having satisfied himself that he had sufficiently analyzed the matter, Sean turned his attention back to the conversation going on around him, afraid that he might have missed something important during his distraction but certain he would be able to catch up. Being brilliant had its advantages.

Sean readjusted the cuffs of his sleeves, a mechanism that had served him well since his early school days to signal to his brain that a new topic was to be concentrated upon.

"Good of you to rejoin us," Roderick murmured to him, making Sean jump with a feeling of guilt. He tried to hide it from his friend but must not have been completely successful. Roderick's lopsided smile only held amusement.

"I've known you a long time. I know your tells," the other man reminded Sean, making him feel sheepish for a brief moment.

Sean shrugged off the feeling without moving a muscle. He had already turned his attention to what the women were discussing.

"I will do my best to get any paperwork I might have pertaining to settlements and properties and whatnot. But could you tell me what exactly I should be looking for? There is likely to be any manner of useless items lying about as well. And I cannot bring the entire contents of my late husband's library without causing concern amongst the household."

Lucy was watching her guest closely, Sean could see. Studying her much like some of the other fellows did who studied botany or animal husbandry. Sean would squirm under that scrutiny if it were directed at him. He was impressed by Lady Evangeline's cool demeanor under the pressure.

"What would it matter to the household?" Lucy asked. "And do you mean the servants who would be directed to pack it for you? Or someone else?"

Sean watched as the beautiful young widow swallowed convulsively, the only indication that she wasn't as calm and collected as she appeared. Her gaze never faltered and her hands remained still and composed where they sat in her lap. Sean wanted to get up and pace from just witnessing the tension vibrating the air, but Lady Evangeline didn't even bat an eyelash.

"My late husband's family lives in my home. Or rather, they claim that it is their home and that I am there as their guest. They are quite likely to object to my removal of anything from the premises. And might protest my visit here, as well."

Evangeline made the admission in a tone that did not betray the least qualm despite the likelihood that she was distraught or nervous or something. Sean could see a pulse beating so rapidly in her neck as to be nearly a quiver. He knew she was not as indifferent as she portrayed. His admiration climbed. But he wished to know her thoughts.

He wasn't left wondering about Lucy's thoughts.

"But what business is it of theirs? Even if what they say is true and your home is in actuality theirs, why should they care what you do with your time? And with your husband's possessions, for that matter."

"Well, you see, if the home is theirs, then the contents are theirs as well, don't you see? And my actions reflect upon them."

Lucy's eyebrows rose, and she pulled herself to her full height despite her seated position.

"You are a lady. Nothing you do could possibly reflect poorly on them. And reflect for whose consideration, might I ask? Who do they think might look at you and judge you, or them, poorly? Their associates or your own? Because, surely, they aren't one and the same."

"Lucy," Roderick said the one word, and Sean was surprised to see Lucy blush fiercely.

"I'm so sorry, my lady. I allowed my feelings to get the better of me. It isn't for me to speak ill of your family. I haven't even met them. That was poorly done of me."

To Sean's surprise, Lady Evangeline's laughter peeled out in a pleasant chime.

"I appreciate your defence of my position, Lucy, but I can assure you, I am not being abused in a harmful sense. I would like to change my circumstances, if possible. But if it cannot be done, it won't be the worst thing either. Unless they manage to finagle me into a marriage I don't wish. That will be dreadful. But I am nearly certain I can hold firm."

"Are they trying to force you into marriage?" Again Sean could hear the outrage in Lucy's voice, but she managed not to offer any insult to her guest or her relatives.

"I wouldn't like to use the word force, but yes, they are quite insistent that I ought to wed a nobleman."

"Any nobleman will do or do they have one picked out for you?"

Again, Lady E, as Sean had started to think of her, laughed gently.

"Not just any nobleman, but no, they haven't settled on a specific gentleman. He just has to be an earl or better, since I'm already connected with an earldom."

Lucy was struck silent for a moment with this information. That didn't last long, though.

"But *they* aren't even gentry," she said, clearly confused. "Nor are they your blood relations. How do they think to benefit if you were to wed a duke or a marquis or some such?"

"I can't say that I'm completely clear on that, to be frank. I didn't wish to encourage them by asking questions. Thus far, I have been able to convince them that I am far too saddened by Gerald's passing to even consider remarriage. But that isn't going to hold up much longer since we weren't actually married for that long, and I don't have very good supporting evidence of it having been a love match."

"Was it?" Sean blurted into the conversation before he could think better of it.

Lady E smiled slightly and shook her head almost imperceptibly. "I wish it had been. He was a decent man. But no one appreciates feeling as though they've been purchased much like a horse or some other chattel."

"No, I don't suppose they do," Lucy replied with a slight blush and a quick glance toward Roderick, reminding Sean that Rod had been somewhat a fortune hunter when he had been pursuing his wife.

Perhaps Lucy felt as though she had been the purchaser.

She rallied quickly though. "That is really neither here nor there, I don't suppose, Evangeline. If you don't wish to marry, it matters little what your reasons are. You have done it already. Your obligations are through. You vowed your life to your Mr. Gerald until death did you part. You are no longer obligated to him or his family. We will help you figure this out. You can be sure of that."

With a firm nod, Lucy stood and began to pace about the room, all the better to think, Sean suspected, but he wondered if he ought to get to his own feet since she had stood. Roderick didn't, so he didn't suppose he needed to, but he worried about the finer details.

Roderick was her husband, he might not be under the same obligations as Sean was.

"It doesn't matter if you can't get anything out of the house. It would be better if you could, but if you cannot, we will work with what we have. Do try to find at least your settlement papers. You are entitled to those, for certain. If you cannot find them in your home, your brother ought to have your copy."

When Lady Evangeline made a slight movement, barely anything to signify, Lucy caught herself.

"Ah yes, you did mention you didn't wish to discuss the matter with your brother, didn't you?"

"I would prefer not, but I will beard the lion if I must." When Lucy only looked at her, Evangeline continued, "Winslow has offered repeatedly that I move in with him and his family. It will be his suggested solution to this matter. He might not even give me the papers I seek if he thinks it will contribute toward his ends."

"No, how nefarious!" Lucy gasped.

Evangeline shook her head and waved away Lucy's concerns.

"He isn't actually being cruel or mean, at least not in his mind. He is just a man who thinks he knows what's best for me without thinking to ask for my thoughts on the matter. Or listening when I try to share them," she added with a lift of one shoulder and another slight shake of her head, as though to rid herself of a pesky thought.

Sean was torn.

What could he possibly say to help the poor woman? It forced him to rethink all his thoughts about the gentry.

She was obviously not wicked or grasping. She was just a normal woman with overbearing relatives. Those existed in Scotland as well.

Sean's own dear mother had faced similar or worse treatment. Of course, her situation was exacerbated by her association with an Englishman, but, while not at all the same caliber, it could be compared to Evangeline's marriage to a cit.

He couldn't begrudge her his help.

"Should we accompany you home and help you collect what we will need?" he asked after clearing his throat nervously.

"Oh, no, that would cause far more trouble than it might be worth," Evangeline immediately replied before offering him a sweet smile. "It is kind of you to offer, though, sir, I do thank you. If it comes to that, I will accept the offer. But let us try it the simpler way first."

"Simpler is probably best." Lucy stepped into the conversation briskly. But then she turned to Sean with laughter dancing in her eyes. "But we get anxious to embark on new ideas, don't we?"

Sean laughed and shrugged. There was no argument for that. He wanted to get on with figuring out the lady's dilemma immediately, now that they knew of it. It would drive him mad to wait even the se'en-night that was now planned.

It didn't take long before they were all politely taking their leave of one another, and Lady Evangeline departed with her whey-faced maid in tow. Lucy stood at the door watching the back of their guest's carriage far longer than necessary before she turned to her husband and his friend, her face twisted into an uncharacteristic frown.

"I am worried," she declared unnecessarily. "What if she doesn't come back?"

"She is a grown woman," Roderick started to soothe.

"Who doesn't seem to feel free to make her own decisions or choices."

"It really isn't our affair, my dear."

"It is now," Lucy said staunchly. "And it would have been even if she didn't ask us for our help. I do feel as though I owe her. Her and the others you were considering."

Sean saw Roderick blanch and had to stifle his amusement. He wondered if Roderick had told Lucy all the names from his list. It had been extensive, Sean was sure, since Roderick had always been thorough in his research.

"My dear, you cannot be traipsing about Town interfering in the lives of every woman of means who happened to have been in an unwed state at the same time as you were."

"I don't see why not," Lucy countered.

Sean's chin fell as he watched the dignified young matron stomp away from her husband with her head lifted in a determined set. After a short pause, probably of disbelief, Roderick chased after her. Sean didn't envy either of his friends the conversation he was sure was going to follow.

He turned his attention back to watch what had become of their visitor's carriage. He had to admit, he was intrigued by both the woman herself and her dilemma. It smacked a little too closely to his own dear mother's situation. Although, to be fair, Sean associated everything to his mother. But he had never found an Englishwoman of gentle birth finding herself in a similar state.

That wasn't to say that Lady E had been wed and then deserted intentionally as had happened to the dear Mrs. Smythe. Sean was sure the dearly departed Mr. Gerald hadn't meant to die on his young wife. And really, Lady Evangeline didn't appear to be terribly broken hearted about his death in any case.

Even if she hadn't confirmed it, the marriage was unlikely to have been a love match considering how sheltered the previously impoverished young woman had been and how much older her husband had been. But still, there were similarities he couldn't ignore.

Perhaps it was just the spirit of the matter. But despite her being thoroughly English, Sean would have to help her as best he could.

It was the only right thing. His mother would approve, he was sure of it.

Chapter Five

"Are you in doubt of my loyalty to you, my lady?"

"I beg your pardon?"

Eve had been too caught up in her own thoughts to be adequately paying attention to her maid. But the stiff, aggrieved tone of the woman's voice broke through her preoccupation.

"You have never sent me away to the kitchens before," Gladys sniffed.

"We've barely ever made calls before, Gladys. And you know perfectly well that I have spent precious little time amongst my peers. You have more experience than I do, to be honest. Is it not the done thing? I was certain it must be if Mrs. Northcott suggested it."

Eve paused for a second, allowing that to sink it. It was all true, despite the unadmitted fact that she had been relieved when Lucy had made the suggestion.

"I do apologize if it felt like a demotion. I can assure you, hurting your feelings was never my intention."

"I didn't think it would be, my lady, but it did feel like I was being punished for something I didn't do."

Evangeline's heart was soft despite her efforts to harden it. She had a long history of never relying on nor trusting anyone other than herself. It had served her well throughout her short but dreary, lonely life.

But there was the rub.

Had it truly served her well? Or was it why her life had been lonely? She allowed herself to sigh slightly. Perhaps she ought to reveal her true self to others from time to time and see how that went.

"Why did you ask if it was a question of loyalty rather than of punishment?" Evangeline asked, finally catching up to what had been said.

"Most ladies confide in their maids, my lady. It's one of the comforts of the position, to be frank with you. Being lady's maid is a more solitary position than chambermaid. Not to say I'd like to return to that position, but it was far livelier. No one wants to be friends with the mistress' maid for fear of tattling."

Evangeline couldn't help but laugh over that last statement. She couldn't imagine her very particular maid being one to tattle.

"I got the impression you were going to confide in those people, but you never have in me. And I've known you for more than three years, every single day, my lady." The last bit of politeness was tacked on at the end as though to mitigate the reproachful tone Gladys had been using.

"What made you think I was about to confide in Mrs. or Mr. Northcott?" Evangeline was fascinated by the conversation, unsure what to do with it or where it would lead.

Gladys shrugged. "It was in the air. I know how it feels when someone is about to confide, my lady. You know I've served other ladies before you."

Which was why Gerald had hired the woman to serve his young bride when she didn't enter his household with her own maid, since her father had been far too much of a pinchpenny to hire her one.

Since she had almost never gone out into Society before her marriage, it hadn't really mattered if she had a maid, she was surely capable of doing for herself. But Gerald had insisted and Gladys had joined the household. But the two women had never really become close.

Not that she was close with anyone, in all honesty, Evangeline thought again with a sinking sensation in the pit of her stomach. But since Gerald had hired the woman, surely her loyalties lay with the family and not really with her. Evangeline wasn't sure that she ought to start a quest for closeness with her maid. But she hadn't meant the woman any insult.

"Confiding in anyone when you aren't in the habit is a rather tricky thing, don't you think?" Evangeline finally asked. "Who do you confide in?" she continued, turning the tables on the inquisitive woman.

"Me mum on my day off," the maid answered promptly, making Eve smile.

Having a mother to confide in must be such a comfort. It was one she could barely recall, since she had been quite young when her mother had died in childbirth. Perhaps that was why her father had taken to wasting the estate. He hadn't a steadying hand to assist him nor anyone to confide in.

Eve quickly dismissed the thought. She wasn't in the practice of sharing her thoughts and feelings with anyone, she didn't see how she was going to be able to start now. While she had told the Northcotts a little of her situation and she would have to tell them more when she saw them again, it was the barest minimum to get their assistance. And she was absolutely confident they would not be sharing her secrets with anyone, particularly not the family.

Eve couldn't say the same about her maid on the other hand. That wasn't to say the woman had ever really given her reason to distrust her. But since the family had taken over the running of the house, Eve didn't think anyone considered themselves truly employed by Lady Evangeline, nor did they respect the position she ought to have in the household.

Not to say she wanted to enforce anyone's respect of her position. Not really. It wasn't as though Eve wished to swan around ordering everyone about. But she needed to know her true position, whether or not she had the right to some independence and whether or not she should be having a say in the household.

If she did have the right to independence, she wanted it. Pure and simple.

She didn't want anyone, least of all her dead husband's relatives, telling her what to do. She certainly didn't want to be forced into another marriage she didn't ask for just to solve someone else's wishes or wants.

She knew there were laws against forcing people into marriage. But she wasn't sure how they could possibly be enforced. And the scandal trying to do so would produce might not be worth the effort to Evangeline. But she didn't want to wed upon the command of someone else. Not again.

She didn't wish to wed, full stop, Evangeline reminded herself.

Never mind the twinges of jealousy she had felt when in the presence of the Northcotts. That wasn't for her. There was no way for her to attain such a state. And she wouldn't settle for anything else.

Widowhood was sufficient for her.

Or so she hoped.

That was why she had gone to the strange Scholarly Society on the pretence of visiting Lucy Northcott. She needed to know if any funds she might have were sufficient. She thought the scholars would be able to know what she ought to do. They could surely at least help her with the maths. And with no emotions attached to it.

Of course, Lucy Northcott might wish to attach emotions all over the place.

That seemed to be the woman's skill. But Evangeline would have to resist her new associate's efforts. Could she say her new friend? That was obviously what the other woman wanted, but Eve didn't see how she could really consider Lucy to be her friend.

Oh, not for the reason Lucy might think, Eve dismissed the thought. She hadn't truly even thought of Roderick Northcott's very fleeting interest in her as his courting of her. And she wouldn't have wanted that courtship anyway.

She had less than zero interest in attaching herself to a powerful Society family like the Northcotts. She wouldn't mind accessing the power part, if need be, but the thought of being permanently attached to a family like that made her stomach clench with nerves.

Suddenly, Eve realized she still hadn't really addressed Gladys' statement or concern or whatever she ought to call what the woman had said. Her mind had drifted. Now what?

"My apologies, again, Gladys," Eve began with what she hoped was a gentle, sincere smile. "My mind chased itself all over the place after your last words, and I lost track of our conversation."

The maid frowned a little but nodded. "Of course, my lady, no apology required."

"When you said you confide in your mother, it made me miss mine, but I barely remember her, so it was a distraction."

"Of course, I'm sorry, my lady, that was not well done of me."

Eve had to laugh over that. "That was surely not your fault. Anyone who still has a mother ought to be happy and proud of that fact. And it's hardly your fault that I do not."

Silence lapsed between them for a moment while Evangeline squirmed with discomfort.

"What sort of things do you think I ought to discuss with you that I haven't done?" she finally asked, wondering if she were going to have to ask Gerald's brother to replace the servant for her. But she would trust a new servant even less than she did Gladys. At least Gladys had been with her before the family took over.

"I would think you would want me to find out things about your husband's family, to be truthful with you, my lady. I can't rightly say why you haven't done so yet. I truly would have thought you were somehow oblivious to the situation if not for today's excursion."

Evangeline stared. What could she say to that?

"What about today's drive made you think differently about anything? And what do you know of a situation that I ought to know?"

"You hardly go anywhere but to gardens, m'lady. As you said, you never make calls. You almost never go to Society events. But you did recently. And the papers listed who was in attendance at the ball you went to. And those people were on that list."

"But what makes you tie all these events together? What makes you think my visiting Mrs. Northcott has anything to do with the family?"

Gladys shrugged. "If I were you, if I might be so bold, the family would be the thing uppermost on my mind."

Evangeline wanted to laugh again, not that there was anything really amusing in the experience. But she had thought she was so terribly subtle, and here she was as transparent as bath water. It was the sort of thing that could turn a woman's mind, she suspected. Or annoy her to the point of madness.

In that moment she longed for her old governess. The one her father had sent away when he'd first reduced the family's accounts. Miss Penny had been a delightful companion to her young self, but she had also taught her how to lose herself in a good book. It didn't even have to be fiction. Evangeline loved words and adored learning. Really, nearly any book would do.

But she hadn't brought a book on this infernal drive. The family frowned upon her love of reading. Even Gerald had thought it beneath her, but he hadn't tried to prevent her from reading, unlike his family after his departure. They had actually removed just about all the books from the house. It had nearly broken Evangeline's heart.

"You could get me to find books for you, too, if you had a mind to it."

Was the servant reading her thoughts now? Evangeline startled. "What would make you suggest that?" she asked, finally allowing herself to frown in earnest.

"Wasn't that a scholarly society we just visited? I might be just a servant, but I know who we visited. Or have heard about them, in any case. The servants were right chatty in the kitchens. Nothing out of line was said, though, of course, my lady," she quickly added when Eve's frown must have deepened further. "But the cook and maids had plenty to say about all the experimenting going on around them. Makes it a little hard to keep some of the servants, it sounds like."

Gladys snorted a laughing snicker about that before continuing. "Made me remember when Mr. Robertson took away all the books and how stricken you seemed for it for a brief moment. You always hide your feelings well, but I've learned to read some of them. It was obvious you were disappointed. Your visiting these people today reminded me. I should have offered back then, but you might have been less inclined to accept then anyway. Now I thought you might be more open to such a suggestion."

Evangeline stared at her maid for a moment in silence before asking, "What would the family think?"

"I don't rightly know why you would care what they think, my lady," came the staunch reply from Gladys.

"If they found out, they might turn you off without a reference."

"Only if you let them, and you don't seem the sort to allow the injustice."

"Do you think I could stop them?" Evangeline was growing fascinated by the conversation. Either her maid was a gifted actress or she was genuinely committed to being Eve's maid rather than a lackey for the family.

"Wouldn't you at least try?" Now Gladys was starting to frown. "I suppose I have let my tongue run away with me in this whole conversation, and I ought to apologize or accept my dismissal, but I just thought you seemed ready to make some changes."

Evangeline straightened in her seat and lifted her chin.

"You are right, Gladys. I am ready to make changes. I thank you for bringing some things to my attention. And I apologize that I haven't been more friendly with you before now. You are right," she admitted, her tone turning apologetic. "I have held your loyalty in question. I considered everyone in the household to be loyal to the family."

"I can understand why you would think that, my lady, but I'm sure almost everyone would be loyal to you if you were to take a stand of any kind."

Eve could only stare. It was an odd situation to contemplate. If she were able to gain her independence, perhaps she could take some of the servants with her.

A delicious shiver engulfed her. Not at all like the one that had struck her when she'd seen Mr. Smythe. This one was of the independent intelligence variety. But she would still have to contemplate the other very soon.

Take a stand. What seductive words, Evangeline thought with another slight shiver.

Could she do it? Did she want to?

Well, of course she did, that was the reason she had approached the Northcotts and their scholarly society in the first place. She wanted her independence. It was the stand-taking she was uncertain of.

She had never been one to enjoy confrontation. She doubted that was about to change even if she was a widow of means. If it turned out there were funds for her to set herself up, that just meant she had the required circumstances. But getting herself into those circumstances, or exerting them, or what have you, might still be beyond her abilities.

"How do you think the family would react if I were to do something so rash?" Evangeline finally asked the other woman, fascinated by this opportunity to question someone familiar with the situation.

"Badly, I'm sure," Gladys replied promptly. "They will make every effort to control you, just as they have done since your husband passed. It has been poorly done of you, ma'am, to allow it."

Eve could only stare once more.

"I beg your pardon."

What was she supposed to say to such a declaration? Even with servants, she wasn't accustomed to saying her true thoughts.

"I know those are harsh words, and it isn't my place to say them, but don't you agree? Don't you think it would have eventually become easier to keep them in their place if you had started that way from the beginning? Now they have grown accustomed to the situation and are no doubt quite bold about it. They will resist strongly if you try to make any changes to the household now."

Evangeline was left wondering what had happened to her uncomfortable, but ordered, world. Now she was still uncomfortable but it felt as though everything had become messy and out of control.

How had it happened that her cool but polite servant was scolding her? Eve braced herself mentally but then poured as much starch into her backbone and her voice as she could muster.

"I cannot rightly say where your change of attitude is coming from, Gladys, but I would thank you to remember that I am your mistress."

"Of course, you are, my lady, and I truly have meant you no disrespect. And if you hadn't gone to visit those scholar people I would never have said a thing to you. But it seems to me that you are looking for a change, and I aim to assist you with it."

When Eve remained silent the maid wilted a little in front of her eyes but continued speaking.

"You are right, my lady, it isn't my place to point out anything to you, and I should remember that we aren't friendly and are far from equals. But I've admired you for nearly three years now and was that excited to see that you might be ready to burst out of your shell. If you want to turn me off now, I suppose I will understand."

"Of course I'm not going to turn you off. I am merely unused to anyone other than the family speaking to me frankly. And after my experiences with them, I don't find frank speech to be to my liking. But that is misguided on my part, I dare say. And you are quite right. It is time for a change. I appreciate your offer to assist me. I will have to give it a great deal more thought. But perhaps it will help to discuss it with someone."

"I swear to you, I will guard your confidences as though my life depended upon it."

Evangeline laughed a little. She had thought her maid cold and curt, but she was turning out to be dramatic and warm. Far different than Eve was used to, that was certain. But while it would take some adjusting, she quite expected to enjoy the change.

"I doubt it will be life and death matters we will discuss, but I will be counting on your discretion. Especially from the family. That will be the biggest challenge since they seem to have their eyes and fingers everywhere."

Gladys sniffed. "They don't know their place, that's for certain."

Eve laughed again. She never felt light-hearted enough to laugh. It felt strange in her throat. But she was going to thoroughly enjoy getting used to it if it continued.

They set themselves to the task of planning what she ought to do, and the rest of the drive back to London passed quickly.

Chapter Six

Sean stood and strode toward the door when he caught Lucy's speculative gaze fixated upon him. Before he could make good his escape, though, she called to him.

"You will help the lady, won't you, Sean?" Lucy's tone hovered between wheedling and commanding.

With a stifled sigh, Sean turned to his hostess.

"Of course," he answered immediately.

"There is no *of course* about it, Sean, and well you know it. I'm sure you noticed she is quite English."

"It was impossible to ignore, to be sure," Sean countered with a grin, his bur growing stronger for a moment.

"Will that be a problem for you?"

"I'm fairly certain it will be, but that shan't prevent me from helping her."

"Why?"

Sean didn't bother stifling his sigh this time. His friend's wife could be more persistent than a gnat and nearly as annoying when she put her mind to something. It was vastly amusing to watch when it was someone else she was bothering. Not so much when it was himself she had set her sights upon.

"Why are you asking me why I will help your friend? Is that not what you want me to do?"

"Of course it's what I want you to do," Lucy replied firmly and with a bit of a flounce. "But I'm trying to understand you. You made such a to do about my English presence in Roderick's life, which made no sense to me at the time, since it's hard to avoid the fact that Rod is also quite British."

"We're all British, if forced, Mrs. Northcott," Sean said, trying not to growl. "It's the fact that the lad is English that I try exceedingly hard to ignore."

Sean ignored the same lad's bark of laughter and carried on trying to educate the man's misguided wife.

"It's a sad but true fact that the lot of you are English, her ladyship included. But Roderick Northcott has been mighty good to me despite his English hide, so I have given him my loyalty. That extended to you when he wed with you. And now, the two of you have asked me to help this lady. She is very English. That can't be helped or ignored. But she also reminded me of me mam. So while I would have helped her anyway, because you asked it of me, now I want to, and in fact, am determined to do so." He heaved a sigh. "Does that satisfy your curious nature, madam?"

Lucy stared at him in her disconcerting way as though she were examining his very innards. Then her face changed subtly.

"She's a very beautiful woman."

"What does that have to do with anything?" Sean asked with a frown spreading from his forehead down into his core as a sense of foreboding came upon him.

"You aren't starting to play your matchmaking games, are you? Not with me." With dread mounting he turned to Roderick. "You canna allow her to play at such things."

But Roderick just laughed and held up his hands. "You are a man of science, Smythe. You can surely handle a couple of women."

"Not likely," Sean growled. Finally, he ignored how rude it was and he strode from the room without taking his leave.

At times it was a blessing the estate Roderick had bought for their use was so large as it allowed him plenty of room to move around and work out his frustrations.

"Aye she's a fair bonny lass," he said as he stomped down one pathway between the house and a copse of trees. "But that don't mean a thing. She's bonny for an Englishwoman. That's not saying much if one puts too fine a point on it. But bonny is as bonny does. It doesn't mean I aim to be matched with her."

He continued to mutter and stomp for a good while until he had walked around the entire property and ended up back at his small shed.

And this time he would call it a shed. He'd even call it such to her face if Lucy were present.

Maybe not. Despite his being disgruntled with her at the moment, she really was dear to him even if she was English. He wouldn't intentionally upset her.

He traipsed into his – library – and looked around with a proprietary air. It was an excellent space. Lucy had done well in her firm direction of the workmen. He would be able to work out all the calculations for the bonny Englishwoman and her widow's provisions in the bright, roomy place.

With a sound that was half laughter and half growl, Sean shoved his hand through the thick brown waves surrounding his head. He likely ought to lop the locks off. His mam would be disappointed but they weren't of much use to him, causing far more trouble than they were worth, falling onto his forehead and distracting him when deep in thought.

He was certainly distracted now.

With a frustrated grunt, Sean slumped into his seat, but then he quickly shook off the doldrums. He had many equations to work on and it was a worthier pursuit than mooning over a beautiful lady who wasn't for the likes of him.

There was that paper Gauss had sent him. It was surely going to take him hours to decipher since the man always wrote half his drafts in German. But it would certainly be worth the effort required. Sean welcomed the mental acrobatics that were in his future. They would surely chase the Englishwoman from his thoughts until he needed to deal with her.

But even as he examined the astronomer's latest dissertation on quadratic forms and how those relate using whole numbers, he couldn't focus his attention, finding himself rereading the same set of integers over and over. When he realized what was happening, he stood up in disgust, unwilling to so disrespect the learned man's work by such a display of inattention.

If he were going to become even half as successful as Karl Gauss, Sean was going to have to get even more serious about his pursuits. Just looking at the paper the other man was about to publish made him even more determined than ever to make his own discoveries. But he would never be so altruistic as the German scholar.

After his childhood deprivations, Sean had no intention of refusing any lucrative offers sent in his direction. Gauss was noble and principled, but that didn't keep food on his table.

Not that he had serious plans for pursuing family life any time soon, but it might be nice to have a wife and children one day. He had to be able to keep them housed and fed. There was no way he could expect Roderick to support him with a family in tow.

Sean shoved his hand into his thick hair once more, almost getting it stuck in the density, which prompted a laugh as he forced his attention back to the sheet of paper he was scratching on. The symbols and equations danced in front of him for a moment before he narrowed his focus and made order of them once more.

He needed to make sense of his studies or this perfect opportunity wouldn't last. While he trusted Roderick to support him in friendship, Sean couldn't rely on the man to keep sponsoring his studies if he didn't produce some results at least once in a while.

Even though the Northcotts had asked him to assist Lady Evangeline, he couldn't allow thoughts of her to derail his studies. It was what drew him to mathematics in the first place.

There was an order to maths. One plus one always equals two. Well, except when it didn't, but even that was predictable and quantifiable. He needed that order now more than ever.

He could not allow a beautiful Englishwoman to disorder the well-ordered equations of his life. Yet, every time he had to lift his pen to refill the ink, his mind insisted on wandering back to Lady Evangeline and her self-contained, fascinating beauty and obvious intelligence.

The mathematical enigma he was working on lay before him, the numbers should command his complete attention. But as he contemplated the intricate equations, he kept seeing the pulse at the base of the lady's neck, its rapid fluttering the only indication that she was nervous about approaching the Society for help. Even her eyes, usually thought to be the window to a person's soul, only gave away so much. They might be the color of a stormy sea, but they certainly never revealed her true feelings.

The woman fascinated him. That had never happened to him before.

"No," he muttered, shaking his head, his Scottish determination taking over. He tapped his quill against the desk, the crisp sound reverberating through the small room.

He was here to work, to prove his prowess as a mathematician, to show Roderick he was right to support Sean's change of specialty, not to be beguiled by feelings that had no place in his ambitions.

Gazing out his window into the lush greenery of the estate orchard, Sean firmed his resolve. His heart swelled with a mixture of pride and longing. He was a son of Scotland, a land of deep loyalties and a history rich with struggle and perseverance. The ambition to rise above the challenges of his origins and make a name for himself burned within him like a fervent flame.

His wretch of an English father would never win. His claims that Sean was nothing but a waste of time could not be found to be true. He turned his attention back to his calculations, the numbers forming into a marching line that mirrored his determination. Yet, a stray thought crept in – a vision of Lady Evangeline's gentle smile that had peeped out a time or two during her brief visit, a symbol of resilience that defied the complexities of the theorems he was trying to corral.

"Focus, Smythe," he admonished himself in a low growl. He leaned in, squinting at the equations before him, his determination battling against the trickles of distraction that threatened his concentration.

The shadows elongated across the room as the hours passed. Sean's forehead creased in concentration, his fingers smudged with ink, evidence of his dogged pursuit and determination to succeed. He refused to give up despite the magnetic pull that urged him to set aside his calculations and dally in dreams and longing.

As the sun finally slipped beyond the horizon a persistent knock at his door pulled him from his preoccupation. It was a footman with his correspondence as well as a reminder of Lucy's insistence that he attend the gathering for the evening meal.

Sean leaned back in his chair, his breath heavy with both triumph and fatigue. The equations were finally in order, the solution elegantly revealed. His sense of accomplishment was tempered by the fact that it should not have taken him the entire day to figure out. But he had persevered and for that he had to be satisfied.

He turned to the papers the servant had delivered. Another letter from Carrick, Viscount Harlowe. *When will the man let it go? Can't he accept I want nothing to do with any relatives of the man who sired me? I'd consign the entire English race to perdition if not for the fact that Roddie proves they can't all be evil. But surely if Viscount Harlow is a relation to the viper who sired me, there can't be much good in him.*

With that, Sean tossed the letter, unopened, into a drawer, ignoring the pile of envelopes already in there. If he had any sense, he'd throw the lot in the fire, but he couldn't quite bring himself to do that. With a shake of his head and without a backward glance, Sean shoved his arms into his jacket as he strode from his shed.

Chapter Seven

Evangeline swept into the house with her head up, her body stiff, and her maid properly in tow. The butler bowed over her hand very elegantly as he took her hat and outerwear from her before handing her off to a footman who escorted her to the excessive opulence of the drawing room.

Gerald's tastes had reflected his newfound wealth, that was certain, Eve thought as she tried not to wrinkle her nose when she looked around the too bright room. The late afternoon sun reflected in a less than favorable manner on all the gilt-encrusted furniture scattered about the cluttered room.

She much preferred to spend time in the small salon that had managed to escape her husband's remodelling fervor, but the family preferred she spend her time here, in the opulence, where they could stare at her as their prize, much as her late husband had been in the habit of doing.

Eve had tolerated it from Gerald as he had rescued her father from penury and she felt it her obligation since she had taken vows with the man. She had not vowed anything to his family, so it was far more difficult for her to stomach.

But today it was all much worse than usual. After her visit to the pleasant but simple elegance of the smaller home the Northcotts occupied on the lands of their scholarly society, Evangeline found the contrast with her place of dwelling was far from favorable. For one thing, the memories of her brief and unfulfilling marriage seemed to linger in every corner, a constant reminder of the life she had been forced into.

Well, forced was too strong, of course. No one had held a weapon upon her. But how was she to say no when her father alternated between haranguing her and weeping over her? And then there had been her brother. He had insisted he would never ask it of her but reminded her of how desperate he was to restore the estate before he could wed.

Evangeline fidgeted on the uncomfortable settee. These were old issues. The matter was past. She had wed Gerald. And now Gerald too was passed, as was her father.

She needn't dwell on the whys and wherefores of how she ended up in the situation in which she found herself. Even the uncomfortable marriage she had endured didn't matter, aside from the fact that it reinforced her determination to resist the family's efforts to marry her off to the nearest nobleman.

Her maid, Gladys, stood by her side, offering a now reassuring presence. After the long drive in which they confided in one another for the first time, Eve didn't resist the other woman's watchful attention. It might still be odd that the family expected her to be escorted, even within her own home, but it was far less oppressive to her now.

Evangeline gazed out the window, her thoughts drifting to the enigmatic mathematician who had promised to help her. She found herself drawn to his intellect and the spark of independence he seemed to possess—a trait she desperately yearned for.

As she contemplated her newfound path toward financial independence, she couldn't ignore the whispers of her husband's family echoing through the halls. Oh, of course they wouldn't actually whisper, they were far too crass for that.

They loved to shout. Especially Ralph, Gerald's younger brother. But the shouts seemed to echo long after they had ended, following her from room to room like a constant hum.

It was as though Ralph were still in competition with the shadow of his older brother. He tried to be bigger, louder, and more brash than even Gerald ever could be. And then there was Ralph's matronly wife who considered it her duty to guide and direct Evangeline in all things.

It never ceased to amaze Eve that Sabina thought to tell her how to go on in Society. It was unfortunate that the pair of them had taken on the running of Gerald's bank. They didn't have Gerald's know-how and they were sure to lose their noble clientele if they didn't stop trying so hard to socialize with them.

"Ah, you have returned," Sabina stated the obvious as she moved her large frame into the room, her gabardine gown rustling heavily with every laboured step. "You were gone a long while," she complained in a grating tone.

"Did we have an appointment I forgot about?" Eve asked knowing full well there had been nothing planned for the day.

"No." Eve could see the other woman was reluctant to admit. "No, nothing was arranged. But one of the gentlemen from the bank stopped in for tea. It would have been nicer if you had been here to entertain him."

Evangeline turned her face back toward the window. How was she to answer such a statement?

Sabina hadn't mentioned which particular gentleman, so it must not have been one of their more noble clients or she would have been crowing about the coup of having him visit their home. And she would have been berating Eve rather than just bemoaning her absence.

"I'm surprised you enjoy conducting business in your home," she finally commented as gently as she could.

Sabina, for no reason Eve could understand, considered herself an expert on polite behaviour, often trying to direct Eve's words and actions while interacting with other members of the *ton*.

Not that Evangeline considered herself to be a true member of High Society. She hadn't even made her curtsy to the queen before she married Gerald. It was only his money and a distant cousin's patronage that arranged it for her soon after her wedding.

And now, she had only just started attending a few events here and there. The ones that seemed like they might be interesting or if she felt a particular obligation because they were some sort of connection of hers. She resisted any suggestions from Sabina. And absolutely refused to discuss any of Gerald's businesses whenever she was out.

She still didn't understand much of Gerald's business connections although that was slowly changing. Ralph and Sabina didn't suffer from the same misapprehensions as Gerald had that she was too pretty to bother thinking.

They were forever trying to discuss shipping or manufacturing or banking with her. Eve couldn't understand why they were always yammering on about it with her.

It wasn't really as though she wasn't interested in such things, nor that she knew nothing on the subject.

It was that she didn't wish to discuss it with them. She suspected they thought Gerald had confided in her in such matters and she might be privy to some secret to success that they couldn't discover on their own. It was certain Gerald had never shared his business acumen with his brother.

And from what Evangeline could understand, Ralph and Sabina were not doing nearly as well as Gerald had.

Her wandering thoughts were brought back into focus when Sabina started to protest.

"It isn't conducting business when it's over tea, my lady," Sabina said, insisting on the polite address but ruining it with her snide tone.

Evangeline kept a pleasant smile upon her face with considerable effort.

"My mistake, then," Eve answered in a mild tone that she knew irritated her sister-in-law. "Perhaps Gerald never had his clients here for a different reason."

This stirred up Sabina's ire in a much different way. It appeared as though Eve had slapped her, which was so far from the truth as to be farcical.

"Are you quite certain he didn't?" the irate woman finally asked.

"Quite certain. But if you don't believe me, you could ask the servants, I'm sure. I understood Gerald quite prided himself on not mixing business with pleasure as he termed it. But I might have been mistaken, of course."

Eve finalized her statement with a gentle smile. The one she knew Sabina both adored and loathed, much to Eve's bewilderment.

"Well." Sabina said it in a breathy, irritated manner, but didn't seem to have anything else to add.

"Was your caller accompanied?" Eve finally asked, having no desire to torture the other woman even if it was perhaps deserved.

"Accompanied? No, it was just Baron Heath. He told Ralph he was only in Town for a week to see to business so Ralph invited him."

Evangeline relaxed slightly. She was reasonably sure the baron was married with several young children, so not someone the family would be pushing her to marry.

"That was kind of Ralph," Eve said but had to add, "although Heath would have likely enjoyed an invitation to one of the clubs even more."

"You well know Ralph isn't a member of any clubs." Sabina was back to being irritated and Evangeline was immediately contrite.

"I truly forgot, Sabina, I do apologize. It was just where Gerald always took any clients when he most wished to extend hospitality. Or even a pub by the docks if it was a shipping customer. I meant no insult to Ralph. I was merely thinking of alternatives to bringing them home."

"Ralph knows I like to be involved," Sabina replied with a pious tone that quite belied her mercenary air.

"Quite," Evangeline finally managed to choke out in as normal a tone as she could muster.

The family was fascinating to her when she wasn't inwardly cursing them to perdition. She doubted she would ever understand them.

Despite their near constant efforts to control her, Evangeline couldn't despise them. Ralph's willingness to include his wife in his business efforts was admirable in an age where women were expected to remain beautiful decoration whose only pursuits were within the home. He even tried to discuss such matters with Evangeline, but she had complicated feelings about the business dealings so she never engaged with him despite her curiosity.

Perhaps she ought to take an interest.

It would be the perfect way to search for the papers she would need for Mr. Smythe to assist her, she realized with dawning delight, hoping her excitement wasn't suddenly written upon her features.

"What sort of business was the baron conducting in Town?" Eve asked. "Are all his interests with Robertsons?"

"Mostly just the bank. But Ralph is hoping we might buy part ownership of the man's mines."

"Oh, is Heath looking for investors?"

"No," Sabina sighed. "But we need the ore."

Evangeline wasn't completely certain of the connection but decided she had demonstrated enough interest for the time being. Sabina wasn't stupid enough not to notice a sudden about face in Evangeline's attitude toward business if she were to show too much interest at once.

"How was your visit?" Sabina finally asked, after a silence had lapsed between them, clearly trying to play nice.

"It was quite enjoyable," Evangeline was able to answer with complete truth. "It was a fine day for the drive, and it was pleasant to have a little visit with Mr. and Mrs. Northcott."

"Aren't they getting themselves caught up with the fringes?" Sabina asked, ignoring the fact that she herself was doing much the same when she socialized with bank clients, or even worse from a societal point of view.

Evangeline didn't so much as twitch in acknowledgement of her amusement.

"I didn't notice anything untoward," Evangeline replied mildly.

"I suppose one of Everleigh's sons would have to be fully acceptable," was Sabina's begrudging acknowledgment, to which Eve merely murmured something that sounded like agreement. "But what could you possibly have to talk about with such ones?"

Eve forced a light laugh. "My dear Sabina, Lucy Northcott has been about in Society since she was barely out of the schoolroom. She knows everyone. Her sister-in-law is one of the most active members of Society, so Lucy keeps herself well informed of all the goings on. Despite their isolated location, I could find out more from her than from visiting many of the withdrawing rooms of Mayfair."

Eve wasn't about to tell Sabina about the scholars and how fascinating all their studies were. It wasn't likely to interest her for one thing, but for another, Eve could only imagine the efforts Sabina and Ralph would go through to prevent her from going again. And Eve was determined to keep her plan to return to the estate and learn more.

It had nothing to do with the handsome Sean Smythe. The thought popped into Evangeline's mind only to be quickly dismissed.

She shouldn't even have to remind herself of that. There was no accounting for the strange thoughts that flit through one's head. She gave hers a small shake to return it to the matter at hand.

Sabina was talking about some new crisis in the house. For a little over two years, the running of Gerald's house had been Evangeline's responsibility. Eve had quite enjoyed the tasks involved in doing so. But for reasons that were never fully explained to her, upon his death, Sabina and Ralph moved into the mansion. At first, during the initial shock of her husband's sudden death, Evangeline thought it was kindness motivating them to take over everything.

Ralph, of course, took over all the businesses. Eve wasn't at all surprised. Despite Gerald's very well publicized low opinion of his brother's intellect, he had also been very clear about his thoughts on a woman's abilities and intellect, so Eve would never have thought he would entrust anything to her. But the house had been her domain.

Gerald had seemed to appreciate her efforts there. Even though theirs hadn't been a love match in any way, it still hurt her feelings that he hadn't arranged for her to keep her house.

Perhaps she should follow Sabina's urgings and remarry. At least then she would have her own home once more. But she didn't want a husband to come with that house. Which was why she had spoken with the Northcotts and their economist. She needed to find the paperwork they had told her about.

But how to do so without Sabina and Ralph or one of their nosy children preventing her?

Evangeline couldn't help the puff of disappointment that escaped her. Of course, Sabina nearly pounced upon her.

"You've gone and exhausted yourself with your visit, haven't you?"

"Not at all," Eve returned in as mild tone as she could manage, avoiding looking toward Gladys for fear her face would reveal her true feelings. "I was just thinking about Gerald."

Eve didn't use this stratagem often, but it always worked. Sabina was always stopped in her tracks when he was mentioned. It was as though, even from death, he was more powerful than everyone else. Eve might not have been in love with her husband, but she couldn't help but admire his strength.

"Of course," Sabina choked out.

"I think I'll go spend some time in his library. It's where I always feel closest to him."

"Of course," Sabina said again, this time a little less choked but even more restrained.

Eve knew the other woman would want to stop her but couldn't. Eve reminded herself that gloating was beneath her as she drifted from the room. It would also give away her scheme. Eyes downcast and her pace slow, Eve made her way out of the drawing room. Gladys followed close on her heels.

Chapter Eight

"That was terribly wise of you, my lady," Gladys complimented in a bright but low voice.

"Thank you," Eve whispered back, keeping her grin contained lest one of the footmen were to remark upon it to Sabina. "Hopefully we'll get at least a little bit of privacy. But we can be certain Clifton or Richard will be along at any moment."

"Those ones," Gladys said with a contemptuous sniff.

Evangeline didn't disagree, but she wouldn't disparage her nephews out loud. Gerald had thought his brother's sons were completely useless, and Eve couldn't argue the fact, but she suspected they had never been provided any appropriate guidance. Really, shouldn't their uncle have done so if he thought so little of their father?

Gerald had never agreed with her assessment of the situation nor had he entertained her opinions on what to do about it. Now he was gone and his nephews were as bad or worse than their parents, trying to control Eve's life and seemingly making every effort to ruin the businesses they had taken over upon their uncle's death.

Eve thought about the last conversation she'd tried to have with the boys when they had been trying to tell her what to do.

"You don't eat enough," Clifton had said with a frown.

"That isn't what you said last week," she had countered in as mild tone as she could manage when what she really wanted to do was throw her plate at the young man.

"That was different," he said with a petulant pout. "Sweets will only make you ugly."

"Is that what happened to you?" Richard asked his brother with a raucous guffaw as he aimed a punch at his older brother's beefy arm.

In an effort to divert their attention away from their constant bickering, Eve asked about their recent efforts at Robertsons.

"How are you managing at the shipyard? Will you have the latest finished and ready to sail before the gales turn?"

Eve had thought it was a reasonable question. It was a reasonable question. One that anyone could ask. But it had prompted an even more negative reply from her nephews than she could have expected.

"You know nothing about gales, nor about ships, my lady," Richard sneered.

"Your only task is to sit quietly and look pretty," Clifton added, for a moment in harmony with his lout of a brother.

It wasn't going to do her good to think about that memory, but it had hurt at the time and it still stung. She had been trying to be kind to the overgrown urchins. They had not returned the favour.

Eve sighed. Of course, no one would have expected her to take over any businesses, but she suspected she might do an acceptable job of it. Better than those two at any rate. She had certainly absorbed enough information from her husband when he had talked about his business practices every day of their short marriage.

The fact that he had told her things in an effort to demonstrate how much more intelligent he was than her didn't negate the fact that he had told her many of his business stratagems. Too bad the family wouldn't listen to her when she tried to explain that to them.

After her first initial attempt went so badly, she refused to rise to the topic when they brought it up. She had quickly given up on that effort and learned to tune them out when they talked of such things.

While they claimed to want to know what Gerald had said on certain topics, they wouldn't actually listen to any advice she had to offer, so she refused to make the attempt. Perhaps that was selfish on her part, but if they only wanted to hear what they wanted to hear, she couldn't pander to such faulty thinking.

Pushing the unhelpful thoughts aside, Eve hurried to the large desk that sat almost in the middle of the room. After staring at it for a brief moment, she shook her head. Surely her settlement papers weren't so important to her husband that he would keep them in his desk.

Where would *he keep them?*

Asking herself didn't shake the answer loose. She would just have to search.

If only she could ask the family. They were likely to know. She was reasonably sure they had gone through every scrap of paper in the entire house in the days after Gerald's death.

Those days had all been a blur for her. She had been exhausted from caring for her husband in that final fortnight of his life. It had been a shock to everyone that someone who had previously held such vitality could just disappear like that, and so quickly.

The man might have treated her as a simple-minded possession, a deeply disappointing possession at that when she hadn't become pregnant with an heir for him, but still, he had never beaten her, and he was worthy of respect, even in his death.

Evangeline couldn't believe how quickly the family had taken over everything. Somehow it seemed disrespectful of them.

At first, she hadn't even thought to protest. It had seemed like a firm arrangement, as though they had already arranged it with Gerald and no one had bothered to tell her anything.

Of course, no one would bother to tell her anything because Gerald didn't think her capable of understanding his business, despite his penchant for telling her everything. But he had talked to her enough about his various business interests as well as his very strong feelings about his family's lack of ability when it came to those businesses that Eve was surprised he would leave the decision making up to them.

He would never have left it up to her, either, she was sure, so that was never in question. It was just her surprise that Ralph was to take over everything that gave her pause at all.

That and their immediate involvement in every aspect of her own life.

She ought to be grateful they hadn't put her from the house rather than thinking uncharitable thoughts about them, Eve reminded herself as she swallowed another sigh. If she wasn't careful Gladys was going to try to make her swallow a tincture for all the sighing she'd been doing.

"Have you thought to look through the book case, my lady?"

It was as though her thoughts had conjured the woman. Eve nearly jumped from her skin.

“I’m so sorry,” Gladys exclaimed. “I didn’t mean to startle you.”

“Quite all right, Gladys, I was merely allowing my thoughts to wander, which, considering the limited time we likely have, was rather foolish of me.” Eve laughed a little. “To answer your question, though, no, I didn’t think to look in the bookcase. Would you like to do so while I continue with the desk?”

Eve's gaze drifted over the cluttered shelves as Gladys approached them, where leather-bound volumes on trade and navigation sat beside oddly ornate texts about ancient libraries. She had never understood Gerald's fascination with lost knowledge, particularly his collection of books about Alexandria.

"Think of it, my dear," he would say, tapping the spines of his prized volumes with an oddly reverent touch, "the greatest repository of knowledge ever assembled, lost to time."

Now as she searched for her settlement papers, her fingers brushed past similar books shoved into various drawers in the large desk. One particularly worn tome caught her attention - its spine marked with an unusual series of numbers rather than a title. But she couldn't afford to be distracted by Gerald's peculiar interests now.

“I would be happy to help in any way.”

Gladys set to work immediately, concentrating her efforts on the bottom shelves.

“No one is likely to look here, is my way of thinking,” she explained as she started rummaging.

But why would her settlement papers be put where no one would look?

Evangeline didn’t think they were that big of a secret. They likely weren’t a secret at all. She just didn’t know what or where they were. But that didn’t necessarily mean there was anything questionable involved in her lack of knowledge.

She hadn't asked and no one had told her. That was the extent of it. She should have asked to see them when they had been signed originally. She wouldn't feel so ignorant in this moment if she had.

Gulping down her disappointment in herself, Eve became engrossed in the contents of her late husband's desk, thrilled that it seemed to have been left exactly the way Gerald had left it the last time he sat there. It was odd that his desk be so untouched, considering he had been gone more than a year. Especially considering the family's touch was felt in every other part of the house. Eve was still surprised she hadn't been asked to vacate her chamber. She had been allowed to remain in the room adjoining Gerald's. Ralph and Sabina had yet to take over the suite of rooms.

Eve reminded herself to be grateful for such mercies.

But then she heard the approach of heavy footsteps. She was able, in the blink of a moment, to slide the drawer closed and lean back in the big chair without even a squeak. Gladys was not so lucky.

"What is going on in here?" Richard, Ralph and Sabina's son, nearly bellowed.

Eve allowed her eyebrows to raise in question. "Whatever do you mean?"

"Why are you in here? And why is your maid snooping?"

"I am in here because it makes me feel close to my late husband," Evangeline said in a tone full of dignity. "And Gladys isn't snooping, she is looking for something interesting for us to read together that we haven't yet enjoyed. I seem to have run through the few books in my possession."

He appeared skeptical over her words. "You know you shouldn't really be in here. At least not without one of us to make sure you don't mess anything up. You shouldn't interfere in matters of which you have no understanding."

It took considerable effort not to snort with her feelings about Richard's understanding. Gerald had ranted frequently about his younger nephew's lack of intellect.

Of course, Eve acknowledged, that was Gerald's opinion. It was entirely possible the boy had hidden depths of which they weren't aware.

She hadn't found them in the year since they had been in residence, but it was still possible that she hadn't looked hard enough. That thought helped her to restrain her initial reaction to the young man's rudeness and she was able to offer him a calm reply.

"I appreciate your concern for my husband's affairs, Richard, thank you for the reminder to be careful in here. We shan't be much longer."

She added a gentle smile, hoping he would take it as the dismissal it was intended to be so she could continue in her quest, but she wasn't to be so fortunate.

The dratted man stood in the doorway with his arms crossed, watching them as though he expected them to throw a fit of hysterics in the overly furnished room. Eve considered trying to wait him out, but she doubted she had the patience for an exercise that had such a high probability of a lack of success.

After allowing enough time to pass to demonstrate the boy had no power over her, Eve stood gracefully from the chair that had always been Gerald's domain. Because the family had so rarely visited during his lifetime, it was unlikely they would know that she had never been allowed to sit in that chair before.

It felt like a small rebellion, but it gave her a sense of control that was sadly lacking in her life.

Gladys followed Eve's example after pulling a book from the shelves to match with the excuse Evangeline had provided her nephew. When Richard saw they were doing as he wished, he softened his stance, suddenly realizing he might have overstepped his bounds.

"Are you sure you should be reading? You mustn't overtax yourself, Aunt," he said in a condescending tone that set Eve's teeth on edge. "You have been through a shock and you still aren't up to your former strength."

It was ludicrous for the young man to condescend to her considering he was a year or two younger than her. But that was the stance the entire family had taken. All their actions were in the guise of demonstrating their deep concern for her welfare. Their demands on how she spent her time, who it was spent with, and their efforts to find her a suitable new husband, all purported to be caused by their abiding wish to care for her.

Eve didn't buy it for a second, but she couldn't put her finger on why. And if their intentions weren't sincere, why were they doing it? She still didn't have an answer to that question. She didn't have an answer to most questions. And she was nearly ready to scream about it.

"It was a shock, you're quite correct. But it has been over a year, now. It is time for me to exert myself, at least a trifle, wouldn't you say?"

"Not at all," the overgrown boy said as he trailed her down the hallway.

Of course, he wouldn't agree. None of them would. Eve fought the urge to yell, keeping her composure. She was a lady after all.

But that was why she had gone to the Northcotts and those dear people had agreed to help her. They hadn't mentioned payment, but Eve expected their assistance wouldn't be free.

She couldn't imagine how she would pay them, but that would be part of their assignment, to find her the funds to live her life and to pay her obligations, including to the Scholarly Society.

Chapter Nine

Sean paced around the edges of the fancy library. He had barely just arrived, and already he was restless. He couldn't begin to explain what he was doing in such a place.

While it was true that Lucy had asked him to accompany her, she had asked many times, and he never had accepted before. What had changed?

He refused to acknowledge he was hoping to see Lady Evangeline. Despite the intricate formulas he had been working on for days, thoughts of the lovely young widow were rarely far from his mind. And since she was evidently in half mourning, or perhaps had even left off her mourning all together, there was a possibility she would be present.

But if she were still dressed in grey, he should keep his distance, Sean reminded himself. Well, he ought to keep his distance in any case, whatever the woman was wearing, even if she were to attend the rout.

It was at a rout where he had first made her acquaintance. Or rather, where he had first laid eyes upon her; he hadn't actually approached her or been introduced to her that evening.

He had thought, at the time, that Roderick was going to pursue her, but then Northcott had fixed upon Lucy, and the rest was now their history. He didn't actually meet the lady until Roderick and Lucy's wedding. And had only spoken to her one other time, at that event wherein he had told her he was a mathematician, which had apparently triggered her desire for more information.

Now he couldn't get her off his mind.

What was wrong with him? He had been a very focused scientist for most of his life. Not that he was so very old, but he had been studying sciences since he was twelve. Since he was now nine and twenty, that was clearly more than half his life. And yet, here he was, for the first time ever, struggling to concentrate on his scientific endeavours.

Science was his world. It was the only thing he could make sense of after his father left him and his mother for a proper English bride when Sean was little more than a bairn. Seemingly easily having his Scottish wedding annulled in order to remarry, leaving his Scottish family to deal with the scandal and its implications.

His so-called noble father had been the furthest thing from that description when he left his first wife destitute with a five-year-old to care for.

Sean could never forgive the man. It amused him when Viscount Sutton regularly begged to develop a relationship with him. Amused him and revolted him. Why would the daft man think he would ever want anything to do with him or his tainted title after what he had done to him and his mother?

It wasn't as though Sean could inherit after what his father had done. He couldn't even say what his father wanted of him, since he had never bothered to listen to his entreaties. He didn't need family like that.

He and his mum had been perfectly fine. Well, they hadn't starved at any rate. She had been ruined when her louse of an Englishman had arranged for their marriage to be annulled and she had struggled to keep them housed and fed, but that had only caused a fire to burn within Sean's young heart as he vowed to never conform to the English ways.

And now here he was at a fancy party waiting for a beautiful Englishwoman to show up. He was a fool. She was probably exactly like his father's wife. The proper English wife Lord Sutton had left his Scottish wife for when it turned out he was going to inherit his father's title instead of Sean's uncle who had died suddenly.

Such foolishness.

It was apparently a family trait, Sean realized with scorn as he edged around the room looking for their host so he could make his excuses and leave early. He couldn't stay in this viper's nest a moment longer. He ought to be back at the estate accomplishing something of value rather than slavering over a woman who couldn't possibly deserve his interest.

But there was a stir at the door and the very object of his obsession appeared as though he had conjured her.

She wasn't wearing grey.

Well, perhaps it could be argued that it was a shade of grey. More like a pale purplish colour with a slight grey tint. Sean suspected Lucy would call it mauve or maybe lavender. No, lavender was darker. For a scientist, he was being rather maudlin and romantic all of a sudden, trying to name the colour of a woman's gown. How foolish could he be?

It didn't seem as though she were lacking in funds, though, if she had suddenly updated her wardrobe.

It was a surprise to see her finally out of her full mourning costume. It would seem she had mourned her husband longer than required. Which was respectful of her, of course. Not that Sean wanted any reason to think more highly of her than he had wont to do.

Foolish to read so much into a woman's attire, he admonished himself even as he stood still to admire her. The fabric of her gown looked softer than her full mourning clothing had done. It wasn't just the less severe colour, he was certain of it.

Were women required to torture themselves along with their mourning? The English were even more foolish than he had thought, Sean smiled with the realization even as he couldn't tear his gaze from the vision before him.

She didn't walk, she drifted or floated or some other equally ephemeral verb. He would be turning into a poet next if he didn't stop this foolishness before it could progress.

"Mr. Smythe."

He had drifted into wool-gathering, and now he was caught. The lady was speaking to him.

He nearly started from his skin but managed to bow over her outstretched hand like any other foolish member of Society. His father would be proud. His mother would crow with laughter.

"How delightful to see you, sir," she said when he didn't comment in any way.

"Likewise, I'm sure," he finally choked out. He was surprised when she uttered her little fairy tinkle of laughter.

"You don't look terribly overjoyed to see me, Mr. Smythe. Or is it just social events you don't particularly enjoy?"

"Now why would you go and draw attention to something like that?" he asked, complaining in a good-natured manner, causing her to laugh quietly again.

"Did you find the paperwork you were to search for?" He at least had the wherewithal to ask her in a low voice but not moving too close to her. It would not do to cause the gossips to think they were sharing secrets.

"Not yet," she said. "But I have been finding the search to be ever so fascinating."

"Really?" Sean frowned.

"Mr. Robertson would be appalled to think I was looking at his papers, but they are terribly interesting."

"Are you speaking of the late Mr. Robertson or your brother-in-law?"

Again she laughed, a light dusting of sound that pleased his ears. Sean found he wanted to make her laugh always.

"I suppose neither of them would be too happy with my snooping, but I was thinking of my husband. He didn't think I could understand anything when he told me of his business affairs."

"Why would he bother telling you if he didn't think you could understand?"

"That's a very good question, Mr. Smythe," Lady Evangeline said with a tightening smile as she turned to speak with someone who had approached her, not bothering to even bid him adieu.

Sean had never pretended to understand women, not that he had a great deal of experience even attempting such a feat. But what he misunderstood even more than the subject of women was his own reaction to this particular woman.

Why did he want to follow her and talk to her and listen to her speak and laugh? Why would he want to know her thoughts? Weren't his own thoughts the ones he had always relied upon?

Other people's thoughts had always been a problem for him. Especially English thoughts.

So why would he even consider this Englishwoman's thoughts?

He didn't have an answer to that confounding question but he still found himself overly aware of her presence in the room. Despite his previous intentions to leave the event, Sean found himself still there an hour later when she approached him once more.

"Are you enjoying your evening, Mr. Smythe?"

"Somewhat, thank you. What of yourself?"

"I will admit to you, but please don't tell tales, I still find it strange to socialize amongst the *ton.*"

"Why would that be, lass? Are you not one of them?"

The woman shrugged as though she didn't know or didn't care, Sean wasn't sure which was the case. But she didn't look irritated by his question and for that he was grateful. He didn't know how to get her to elaborate. Blessedly, before the silence grew awkward, she began to speak once more.

"I might have been born to this world, but I never actually inhabited it," she began in a low but not sad voice, as though what she was telling him didn't bother her, but she didn't really want anyone else to hear anyway.

"Due to my father's financial troubles and not having anyone offer to sponsor me, I never made a proper debut until after I had wed Mr. Robertson. And he was quite the contrarian. He loved the fact that my father was an earl, but he didn't really have much use for the nobility, so he didn't care to accompany me to balls or musicales or any such thing. He didn't mind the theatre, so that was where I would do any of my socializing besides morning calls. So I haven't a great deal of practice."

She smiled gently and then turned the tables on him. "What of you? Have you always been involved in Society?"

Sean stared for a moment as though at a loss to how to answer such a daft question, but then he couldn't help but laugh despite her shushing him over the eyes drawn in their direction. But she looked as though she wished to join him in laughter even though she couldn't possibly know why he was amused. He admired her readiness for mirth even more than her beauty. It was a dangerous situation.

"I was born into this world, one could say, but then it was snatched away afore I had even set foot in it."

His cryptic answer caused her face to break out with all sorts of questions written over her features, but she managed to keep her tongue in her head and not ask a single one of them.

He was certain Lucy would have peppered him with those questions if she were in Eve's place. Again, his admiration grew for her and he had to shake his head.

"Perhaps you'll explain that once I've found the needed papers," she said in an almost whisper before she again took herself from his side.

Sean watched her ramrod straight back for a spare moment before he tore his gaze away and finally took his leave of the event as had been his intention more than an hour earlier.

Castigating himself once more for turning into a simpleton over an Englishwoman, Sean took himself back to the estate even as he devised a calculation to determine the number of hours remaining until the woman would follow.

Chapter Ten

It started to feel like a game of cat and mouse. Eve and Gladys wandered through the house trying to avoid any members of the family and even most of the household staff. They could never be sure who would report what to whom.

Sabina expected Evangeline to take tea with her every day and report upon her activities. Those were the most excruciating moments for Eve, as she fought against the urge to tell her sister-in-law just how desperately she wanted out of the household. But Evie was afraid of the consequences if Sabina were to find out what she was planning.

The Robertsons' control over her movements was odd and without an understandable explanation. But Eve was certain it gave them some sort of enjoyment.

"Richard told me he found you in his uncle's library," Sabina commented the day after the incident.

"He did, yes," Eve replied calmly. "Remember, I told you I was going there."

"He thought your maid was going through Gerald's things."

"Did he?" Eve asked. "How very strange."

Sabina appeared undecided but carried on anyway. “You really should keep your focus on social things and leave the house to us.”

Eve couldn’t help it, she had to say something in reply. “Sabina, you do realize that I used to run this house before you moved in, don’t you?”

A frown creased Sabina’s forehead as though she couldn’t understand what Eve was talking about. “It might be better if you didn’t go into the library at all.”

“No,” Eve said. “You have already restricted me from at least half of the house. You cannot prevent me from going into the only room that still feels as though it is Gerald’s,” Eve concluded.

She didn’t think it would make sense for a wife to acquiesce to everything the Robertsons tried to insist upon. Sabina tried to sputter in protest, but Eve didn’t back down.

“I do appreciate the help you’ve extended to me, of course,” Eve uttered the lie without making a face. “But I think you have gone a little too far in the rules you are trying to make for me.”

She allowed the subject to change, but she hoped her point had been made.

Still, it felt as though there were always a member of the family following her around after that. Eve had to rely on Gladys for most of the search as a result. She was nearly despairing over their finding anything before they were promised to leave for their stay at the Northcotts’ home until they finally found a sheaf of papers that showed promise.

As she rifled through another drawer, a sheaf of papers slipped free, scattering across the floor. Eve gathered them quickly, but paused at an odd notation in the margin of what appeared to be a shipping manifest. A sequence of numbers, written in Gerald's precise hand, followed by the words "Alexandria coordinates?" and then crossed out.

She almost set it aside - another of Gerald's peculiar interests - but something about the careful way the numbers had been inscribed made her slip it into the pile she was collecting. She could examine it more closely later, when she wasn't at risk of being discovered by Sabina or one of the footmen.

Eve had heaved a massive sigh of relief to be finally making some sort of progress but then had to quickly shove everything behind a cushion when Clifton strolled into the room and invited her to go for a walk in the park.

It was out of character for Clifton but well in keeping with the family's actions that week. Eve hadn't felt able to refuse. Conversation with her nephew had been stilted and she was glad they had only gone to the small parkette near their house.

“Mother says you aren't supporting her business efforts,” Clifton said cheerfully as they walked with slow steps.

“Did she? How strange,” Eve remarked in a mild tone. “Which efforts would those be? I didn't realize I had been invited to support anything.”

Clifton frowned at her as though confused.

“None of you have struck me as being open to my opinion on anything,” she elaborated.

“Of course not, but Mother wants you to go about more to events and such,” Clifton explained in an overly placating tone that set Evie's teeth on edge.

“Have you any idea how she thinks that would assist Robertsons?”

Clifton opened his mouth but shut it again as though he hadn't an answer.

“Does she think I will procure clientele for the bank or shipping contacts or some such while dancing the minuet?" Eve tried not to allow derision into her tone, but she certainly felt it in the depths of her being.

"You know we've been very patient with you, Lady Evangeline. You ought to show your appreciation." Her nephew finally blurted out these nonsensical words after silence had grown between them and they were nearly returned to the house.

"Thank you, Clifton," Eve said with as much sincerity as she could muster. "I appreciate your attentions in getting me out of the house for a bit."

The young man bowed stiffly and left her without much of a farewell. Eve didn't mind. She hurried back to her room to check on Gladys' progress with their packing.

With relief, Eve discovered that Gladys had been able to rescue the papers she had shoved behind the cushion and packed them at the bottom of the trunk she had been filling with Eve's things for their trip to the country. For that reason, neither of them had been able to take any time to peruse the papers before they arrived at the Scholarly Society.

Eve had barely a chance to glance at the papers before she'd been interrupted, but she was fairly certain some of them might be her settlement papers from what had been written at the top of the first one. Though she hadn't the time to examine them carefully, she was relieved to note that it was unlikely anyone would notice they were missing as they had been shoved into a cupboard that appeared untouched since they had been placed there before her wedding.

She didn't know why she had been concerned the family might prevent her from taking them. It was likely just a habit she had developed to be in fear of them, since they were forever trying to control her comings and goings.

Well, there was reason behind her concerns. They tried to control everything about her life. They expected to vet every decision she made. They wouldn't want her gaining her independence.

And they were not pleased about her proposed visit to the Northcotts.

"Why would you leave Town during the height of the Season?" Sabina had demanded, clearly trying to sound more worried than cross but not truly succeeding.

"What does the Season matter to me? I am far from a debutante seeking an eligible mate. I am a widow."

Evangeline tried to be gentle in her tone, but she doubted she had succeeded. She wondered what Sean Smythe would think of the conversation and nearly laughed at the thought. He would have some caustic remark to make, she was sure.

"But you could remarry," Sabina said. "You should, in fact."

It was a well-worn argument that Eve was used to ignoring. "You are still very young. You surely must want wee ones of your own."

The woman's words caused a clutch in her heart that Eve did her best to ignore along with the rest. She had always wanted children. But one needed a husband for those, and she didn't feel terribly inclined toward having one of those.

Even when she had a husband, children weren't guaranteed. After her own experiences, and from witnessing the uncomfortably warlike relationship that sometimes appeared between Ralph and Sabina despite their seeming partnership, marriage was far from her goal. And Clifton and Richard weren't really a fine testimony of the benefits of having children, she thought with amusement.

"I have no interest in searching out another husband, Sabina, surely you can understand that."

At the woman's irritated huff, Eve softened her words. "Gerald was such a special man," she said.

It was true. He was. Just not in the way Eve might be implying. But she didn't mind being a little flexible with the truth on this subject. She had no intention of wedding, especially not at Sabina's bidding.

"Well, of course he was, dear," Sabina said in the condescending way she adopted when most wanting to affect Eve's behavior. "But that doesn't mean your life needs to end along with his, does it?"

"No, I'm certainly not dead, nor wishing to be," Eve answered, holding onto her composure as tightly as possible, not to give in to the irritation creeping up her back.

"But I also don't feel the need to hurry into another marriage. As you said, I'm still young. I have time to decide if I want to have a family of my own. Or perhaps I can just enjoy being an aunt to my brother's children. And Clifton and Richard will surely wed and have families soon. Their children will need a doting aunt."

Evangeline congratulated herself on the masterful handling of the situation. There was little Sabina could say to argue her points. But she did try her very best.

"The thing is, dear, you really must think of Clifton and Richard. They will be in a much better position to marry well if you do so first."

Eve hadn't been able to do much other than stare at her sister-in-law. She knew she should keep her mouth shut firmly, but she couldn't help but clarify the situation.

"By wed well, do you think to marry the boys into the gentry?"

"Why of course," Sabina replied promptly. "If you were to marry an earl at the very least, then surely their chances will be much improved by being part of your family. Especially if we can get a few more highly placed clients at the bank."

With a weak smile and no further comment, Evangeline finally made her escape and was now tooling along smartly tucked up into the comfortable travelling coach with Gladys beside her and her trunks piled onto the roof and back. Despite Sabina's best efforts, Eve hadn't been prevented from leaving. It had only taken her promise to attend whichever events Sabina thought prudent upon her return.

Eve hadn't been happy about making such an open-ended promise, but if it got her out of the house without any more argument, she had been willing to go to great lengths. She had much to contemplate, though, and was more determined than ever to get herself out of that house and into her own independent life.

She hadn't realized the family expected her to wed in order to elevate their own status for the boys to marry into the gentry. While she had known status was connected to their interest in her remarriage, Eve had actually believed it was out of concern for her own well-being.

Despite her husband's heavy-handed ways, she supposed she had grown used to someone actually considering what was best for her. So even though she hadn't liked most of Sabina and Ralph's suggestions of what she ought to be doing, she had truly believed they had thought their ideas would benefit her.

That had been unforgivably foolish of her.

How could someone so distrustful as she be so silly as to think they were looking to her benefit? Anger began to boil within her. It was far more acceptable to her than the feelings of self-pity that had been swamping her from the moment she'd finally understood.

Thankfully, when it had dawned on her, she hadn't been with Sabina any longer. If Sabina had realized she now better understood the family's intentions toward Evangeline, she might not have allowed her to leave so easily. That thought sent a shudder through her.

"Have you caught a chill, my lady?" Gladys asked, solicitous.

"No," Eve replied with a short chuckle. "Or only in a manner of speaking. A chill of the soul, one could say, if one was being fanciful."

"I didn't think you to be the fanciful sort."

"Neither did I," Eve admitted before sighing. "But it turns out I must be. While I have often lamented the family's controlling ways, I had been under the impression that they were only doing so out of concern for me and my future. Or perhaps just because they like being in control. But now I know that it is for their own futures."

Eve shook her head before continuing.

"The irony is, they are completely wrong-headed in their understanding of the *ton*. Even though I haven't been active in Society, I do know their way of thinking far better than the Robertsons possibly could. Even Gerald knew that. It was the one thing he accepted I might know something about."

"What has happened to alter your understanding of the matter? Was I present and didn't notice?"

This brought welcome mirth to Eve and the laughter she allowed was genuine.

"Perhaps you've always understood their thinking and we weren't yet at the point of discussing matters."

Gladys only continued to stare at Eve, appearing to be at a loss as to what she might be talking about.

"It turns out, Sabina expects me to marry a nobleman with the expectation that I will then introduce her sons to eligible ladies in order for them to make spectacular matches."

Gladys continued to stare, seemingly as surprised as Evangeline had been. "But why would she think a gently bred young woman would wed with one of her rough sons? Surely the wealth isn't that great."

"This is the question I couldn't possibly fathom a guess to answer. I suppose, considering that Gerald married me, they think it possible, even probable. And I cannot argue that. But Gerald was able to cover over any of his rough edges with his fancy trappings and could display to advantage in exalted company. He also had a far better understanding of how to behave than his nephews do. And he had extremely deep pockets. Deep enough to make noble fathers turn their gaze away from his less than ideal lineage. But even if Ralph has inherited all of Gerald's holdings, that doesn't necessarily translate into Clifton or Richard being able to convince a lady to marry them."

"And it isn't likely that Ralph is going to be able to hold onto his brother's wealth, either."

Eve couldn't help an indelicate snort over Gladys' last words. Gerald had seemed quite brilliant to her in his business dealings. She had understood far more than he had credited her with when he was forever droning on about his dealings.

Eve thought he was short-sighted when it came to her, but that couldn't be said about him when it came to anything he thought to invest in. Ralph, unfortunately, did not have his brother's intellectual abilities.

"What are you going to do about her intentions?" Gladys was still frowning.

"They cannot force me."

"They can certainly try," Gladys argued.

"Which is why we are consulting with the scholars to see if they can make sense of my affairs. If I can set up my independence, I needn't be subject to the family's attempts at manipulation."

"Do you really wish to be independent, though, my lady? It doesn't really strike me as something that a properly bred female would wish for."

Suspicions traipsed across Eve's mind with her maid's words. She shouldn't be confiding in anyone. She knew that full well. And yet here she had gone and done so. The thought of forging a friendship had been too seductive. She pressed her lips together to prevent her thoughts from flowing from her mouth while she contemplated her reply.

"I shan't know for sure until I know where I stand. At this point, I don't think independence is anything more than a dream, so there is no harm in finding out." She finally gave a light answer no one could find fault with.

"Of course not. Knowledge is always best," the maid answered promptly, not settling Eve's suspicions in the least.

Eve tried not to be overcome with her disappointment. She had thought Gladys was on her side. But it was possible she was in cahoots with the Robertsons after all, as she had originally thought.

Or perhaps she was seeing monsters in every shadow.

Evangeline huffed a breath, releasing her frustration with effort.

"You don't seem content with this choice," Gladys pointed out.

"It isn't a choice. Not yet, anyway. But I'm not content with the current state of my life. It's time for me to leave mourning behind, but I'm not even sure how many gowns I can afford."

"Can you not just have your bills sent to the offices as you always have?" Gladys' frown deepened.

"I probably can, but I just want to know where I truly stand. Surely there must have been some sort of provision made, wouldn't you think?"

"Of course," Gladys agreed right away.

"The thing is, how awkward would it be for both me and Ralph if he were to decide I had sent too big a bill and he has to deny it? I could never show my face again."

"I would think it's a fairly common occurrence amongst Society ladies. One of the most common pieces of gossip is which lady has outrun her allowance each month."

Evangeline had to laugh over this as it was surely true. Her maid was remarkably well informed. "You seem to know all the gossip," she noted.

Gladys smiled, seemingly proud of herself for this. "I keep my ears open whenever possible."

"What a useful skill," Eve returned without adding anything else.

She couldn't decide if her maid was trustworthy or not. If the woman loved gossip, it was entirely possible she shared as much as she listened. Eve had no interest in being the next topic bandied about.

But she was going to need to learn to confide in people. The entire purpose of her drive today was to tell all her business to the Northcotts and at least one of their scholars with the hopes that they could figure out where she stood financially and maybe even legally.

Did she have the right and the ability to set up an independent establishment? That was the question she was struggling with. Obsessing over, really, considering how many times it popped into her mind.

The question of whether or not she ought to do so was to be left until she knew if it were even possible. But Eve rather thought that if she could, she would.

The possibility of not having anyone to answer to was so very appealing to her.

It was something that men had and didn't think anything of. But it was a rare woman who had true independence. There was always someone who thought it their right to exert control over women and their decisions.

In Evangeline's case there were several. As far as she knew, she didn't have a single possession that truly belonged to her except the locket her mother had given her when she was a little girl and the ring Gerald had given her when they'd wed.

She supposed the clothes she already had were hers outright. But even any future clothes weren't guaranteed under her current circumstances.

"The thing is, I would like to throw off mourning entirely," Eve finally explained aloud. "To do that, I will likely need a completely new wardrobe. I cannot count on the Robertsons paying for it if I don't want to follow their wishes, especially not to wed."

"I can see the truth of your words. There are always strings attached to everything, aren't there?" Gladys replied sagely. "If only you could have taken over your husband's affairs instead of his family overriding you on everything."

"Wouldn't that be lovely?" Evangeline replied in a tone that was wistful even to her own ears. "Gerald didn't trust me to understand much about his business dealings, even though he told me all about them," Eve admitted. "He spent countless hours in that library. Sometimes I'd hear him muttering about maps and ancient texts when he thought no one was listening."

"He was an odd one," Gladys agreed. "Always writing in those leather-bound journals of his."

Eve frowned. "Journals? I haven't seen those since, well, since Ralph and Sabina moved in."

"They're probably still there somewhere," Gladys said. "Hidden away like everything else they don't want you to find."

Eve's breath caught. Something more she needed to investigate later. But first, she needed to know where she stood.

Which was why she was delighted to be arriving at the Northcotts' scholarly estate. Evangeline was exhausted from her own circular thoughts. She needed to know where she stood. And if it required her confiding in others when that had not been her habit since her mother's death when she was twelve years old, then she was nearly certain she could learn how it was done and do a decent job of it.

Evangeline wasn't sure why, but she was convinced she had sufficient intelligence contained in her mind to do whatever she decided, no matter what Gerald or anyone else might have told her.

And she had decided to find out whether or not she owned anything.

Chapter Eleven

Despite feeling more ridiculous than his aunt Franny's Sunday hat, Sean had hovered near any available window nearly all day.

It had been perfectly foolish because, of course, the woman wouldn't arrive in the morning. She had to drive from Town. And sociable women didn't make calls in the morning, even if they were named morning calls.

He should have tried to get something done. Feeling a sense of accomplishment would have set his mind at ease, surely. But how was he to do that when his mind was so cluttered up with thoughts of her?

He had never been so preoccupied with anything that wasn't related to his studies. Even the other scholars had noticed.

Pierce and Ellis had each taken turns making sport of his inability to focus. Despite their fields of study being astronomy and chemistry, they both offered to take the task of helping Lady Evangeline with her economies off his hands.

Even Lincoln had involved himself since he had just returned from visiting the lady's brother, claiming he would now be an expert. They were making a mockery of his distraction. But none of them could understand why it was so very displeasing to him to be so challenged.

Since two of them were legitimate members of the aristocracy and the other had his connections, and all of them fully English at that, they couldn't fathom why he would be so despairing of finding the English rose so appealing.

Sean only hoped they would have the discretion not to say anything to Lady Evangeline when she arrived. That might be a futile hope.

What man could resist ribbing his friend for any reason, but especially such a juicy topic as a devoted scientist becoming distracted by something so nebulous as attraction or feelings?

He could hardly stand it. He had considered leaving the estate for a much-needed visit to his mother in Scotland. But he was still here, pacing before the windows, waiting for the lady to arrive.

Sean assured himself it was merely because he had given his word to Lucy and Roderick, but he knew he was lying. Lying to oneself was beyond foolish. But there he was. Raking a hand through his unruly hair, Sean resumed his pacing, accepting that there would be no calculations taking place that day.

Finally, midafternoon, the crunch of hooves and wheels on the gravel alerted the household to the arrival. At least any members of the household who were attentively awaiting the arrival. Because, really, the horses and carriage didn't make all that much noise.

It took effort but Sean managed not to run out of the house to greet her. It was a close call, though. His brisk walk could almost be called a trot, but at least he wasn't out of breath when he finally arrived in the foyer of the main house where Lucy and Stubbs were directing the footmen about the disposition of the luggage and welcoming their guest.

Even Roderick hadn't arrived in the foyer yet, and surely Lucy would have sent a servant for him as soon as she had heard the arrival. Sean knew she was nearly as anxious as he was about Lady Evangeline's sojourn with the scholars. It was just for a different reason.

Or perhaps a related reason.

Lucy was determined to ensure the woman was provided for because she was rather foolishly ridden with guilt over having wed with Roderick. Since that fine gentleman had been determined to marry a wealthy woman so he could establish the foundation to support his friends' scientific pursuits, he had considered several women as options for matrimony.

Lucy trampled on his plans and wed him herself.

She hadn't been on his list because she wasn't the quiet woman Roderick thought he wanted, not for lack of a large dowry. But everyone could see they were crazy about one another. And now, because she was so blissfully wed, it seemed Lucy felt she had done the other women Roddie had been considering a disservice.

It was amusing to witness, Sean supposed, but he understood enough about feelings and the philosophy of the mind and body connection to know that it couldn't be a comfortable feeling for Lucy even if it was misplaced.

Sean had never been terribly interested in the workings of the psyche but one of the other scholars seemed determined to educate them all on the topic and was particularly intrigued with the workings of Lucy's mind. Sean supposed Lucy was a fascination for them all as most of them hadn't spent much time with females of the species, not even their own family members, since they had all been overlong at school. Blessedly, she seemed delighted to be the object of study rather than offended by the fascination.

But now there was a new, almost mythic, creature on the estate to study. Sean was sure the others would be flocking round before long. Not the least because the woman was so beautiful. If she were as enthralled with their studies as she had professed, the other men would be enslaved much like he was.

That shouldn't annoy him so. But it did. And the others were sure to notice. Sean needed to learn to hide his feelings and reactions better. He needed to think of it as a game of chess. One never revealed one's thoughts and fears while protecting their king.

"Ah, you have arrived," he said inanely as way of greeting. Even he had to roll his eyes over his ludicrous behavior and he didn't blame Lucy in the least for her burst of laughter.

"Never mind the scientists, Evangeline, you will quickly grow used to their strange pronouncements from time to time," Lucy explained as she tucked her arm into the curve of the lady's elbow and escorted her from the room.

With a nod at the lady's maid, Sean fell into step beside her as they trailed behind the two women.

"Was your drive boring?" Lucy was asking with a laugh.

"Delightfully so," Evangeline returned with answering laughter. "Exactly as you'd wish travel to be. I don't usually welcome boredom, but the alternative, while travelling, would definitely be even less welcomed."

"Have you been reading gothic novels, my lady?" Lucy asked, attempting a tease.

Evangeline laughed a little but shook her head. "No, I've once had a broken wheel."

"Oh dear," Lucy said, quickly sobering for a brief moment before another peal of laughter left her. "That can actually turn out romantically, if you can imagine."

"I cannot," Evangeline replied. But Sean could see a smile spreading on her face as she anticipated an amusing anecdote.

"This is how my sister-in-law ensnared my brother."

Sean and Evangeline exchanged expressions of confusion.

"With a broken carriage wheel?" the lady asked with a puzzled frown.

"The very thing to get yourself invited to stay at a gentleman's hunting lodge overnight," Lucy explained with a wide grin. "Then my other brother and I arrived and spoiled the plan a little. But it all worked out in the end. They are delightfully happy and in love. Belle's parents are now trying to work their matchmaking skills on my brother, but Cuthbert has resisted up until now."

Despite her audience's obvious fascination and wish for more information, Lucy clapped her hands and turned the subject. First organizing everything just as she wished, sending the maid off to arrange their guest's quarters and having the footman fetch tea while someone else went to find out what was keeping Roderick.

Sean enjoyed witnessing Lucy's managing ways, but he could see that Evangeline was somewhat shocked by it. Perhaps shocked was too strong a word. Taken aback for certain.

She didn't refuse the cup of tea that was quickly presented to her, though.

"Thank you, this is welcome after the long drive," she murmured.

"Were you not provided with a hamper by your servants?" Lucy asked with a frown.

"I didn't ask for one. I wanted to be away with as little fuss as possible. Sabina was still flapping her hands, trying to think of reasons why I shouldn't leave.

If I had asked for refreshments to be packed, I was certain she would turn that against us in some way and prevent our departure."

"Oh dear, was it dreadful?"

"Rather. And I had to promise to attend whichever event she chooses when I return."

Lucy and Sean both frowned.

Lucy asked before Sean could interject. "What sort of event might she be sending you to?"

Evangeline's sigh was heavy. "I have discovered that she hopes to marry me off to a nobleman so that I can then arrange advantageous marriages for my nephews."

"Your sister-in-law's sons?" Lucy asked for clarification.

When Evangeline nodded, Lucy laughed.

"Does she really believe that is likely to happen?"

"It would seem so."

Lucy snorted less than delicately, revealing her opinion on the topic.

"So it's likely to be a ball or something quite grand, I expect."

"Likely," Evangeline agreed. "I don't truly object to attending a ball. I quite enjoy dancing and seeing all the ladies and gentlemen in their finery, too. But I have no wish to remarry, so it feels rather disingenuous or perhaps even deceptive to attend without intentions."

Lucy nodded slightly but then shrugged.

"I dare say there are plenty of ladies who attend with no intentions. My sister-in-law, for one. And my parents still attend balls now and again. Roderick's brothers' wives adore balls. And every ball has the posse of gossipy older ladies sitting in a corner, don't they? You might have a good time if you forget about the girlish reason younger ladies attend."

Evangeline grinned.

"Perhaps I'll join the posse," she returned lightly.

Sean couldn't help admiring her ability to keep a topic playful even when she obviously had heavy matters on her mind.

His mother would like her. Sean wanted to run from the room at the thought. He also wanted to remain firmly rooted and stare at her for eternity.

For someone intelligent he was acting a fool. But there was little he could do to the contrary.

Chapter Twelve

How was she going to be able to concentrate on the matter at hand? Why was the man she needed help from so distractingly handsome?

Eve did not want to find anyone attractive or appealing. That was surely the way to disaster. Her first marriage had to be her only marriage. And no other type of relationship could be acceptable to her.

Evangeline was shocked that the thought even had to be stated in her mind. Handsome men were not so rare. She couldn't allow one to derail her faculties. He didn't even seem all that happy to see her, so it was ridiculous that his appearance in the doorway had caused her heart to leap.

Could hearts leap?

Perhaps she ought to consult with one of the other members of Northcott's scholarly society. If she recalled correctly, at least one of them was studying medicine and anatomy. Perhaps Eve was actually suffering from some dreaded disease.

Hearts don't leap. And hers certainly hadn't. That was thought with sufficient emphasis that she needn't consider the subject again.

"So tell us what you were able to find," Lucy said, full of excitement and vigour for the project that only filled Eve with nerves.

"I'm not even certain what I found, to be honest. Just yesterday I found a bunch of papers that seem to pertain to me, but I didn't have any time to look at them thoroughly. My maid found a few things, as well. Again, though, because of time constraints and the instinct to hide what I was doing from the family, everything ended up at the bottom of a trunk and we haven't read or looked at it. We were tempted to dig it out and do so in the carriage, but I was too nervous to even open the trunk after having nearly been caught with the papers in the first place. Besides, at that point, it seemed unfair to look without the lot of you."

Lucy's laughter was infectious. If Evangeline weren't so anxious about what might happen to her and her future plans, she might have joined in. But she was in too much turmoil.

After making Sabina the promise to go to whichever entertainment she chose, Eve was more convinced than ever that she needed to get out of that house. And she was here to find out how to make that happen.

"Very well, then, we have something to work with, in that case. Or at least we hope so." Lucy glanced at Mr. Smythe before shifting her gaze back to Eve. "Should we wait until tomorrow morning to get started or do you want to delve in a little bit right away, before supper?"

Lucy broke off with an apologetic expression. "I ought to have mentioned it sooner, perhaps, but we keep country hours here since most of the men prefer working either in the evening or in the early morning but in either case, they don't want to be bothered with mundane matters such as meals. I hope that won't be a problem for you."

"Not at all," Eve said right away. "I prefer country hours myself, so it will be delightful. But since I promised to return home no later than seven days hence, if it wouldn't be an imposition, I would be happy to start right away."

Lucy nodded and then gestured toward Mr. Smythe. "Sean has cleared his schedule as much as he could to tackle this particular equation, and he's here already, so if we fetch your box, we could look at what you brought."

"Gladys will know which one it is," Eve said immediately. "If I could be shown to my room, I will return within a moment."

Before Eve could run from the room, though, Lucy interrupted her steps, turning to Mr. Smythe.

"Sean, would you prefer we work in your library or in Roderick's? Or would it be better to set up here in the receiving room?"

Eve was surprised by the brief flicker of disquiet that covered the man's face before he offered his habitual grin with a shake of his head.

"We shan't all fit in my wee shed, Lucy, and well you know it. At least not comfortably anyhow."

It was clearly a long-standing jest Eve didn't understand, but Lucy returned a sound of outrage that seemed well-rehearsed.

"Sean Smythe, how dare you?" she asked even as she was obviously trying not to laugh. "It's not that small. And it's not a shed. But never mind, I think you're right that staying in the house is best. So Rod's library or here?"

"Here is probably the most comfortable for you ladies," Mr. Smythe began. "But if you have any other callers, it might not remain so private."

Lucy frowned and so did Eve. She hadn't thought of that. It was even possible that Sabina might call. That would sink her ship before it left the harbour, she thought, mimicking one of Gerald's favorite expressions.

"You make a good point, as always, Sean. Could you warn Roderick while I show Evangeline to her room? We will have tea served there when we join you."

It took effort not to laugh over the gentleman's reaction to the promise of tea. It was as though Lucy had promised him gruel rather than roast beef. Lucy must have noticed as well. She didn't try to hide her exasperation.

"There will be biscuits, Sean, have no fear." Lucy turned on her heel and flounced from the room.

Trying not to giggle, Eve followed her.

His rich chuckle followed them out into the hallway. When they were far enough away that he was unlikely to hear, Lucy allowed her giggles to overtake her.

"He is delightful," Lucy told Eve as she tucked her hand into her guest's elbow. "I am sure he will be able to help you and you will have a good time together as you get your life sorted. I do wish you were able to stay longer as I'm not certain we'll be able to find you a new home in merely a se'en-night."

Eve nearly choked. "Oh, no, Mrs. Northcott, Lucy, no, I have no intention of putting that task upon you. I merely wish to know where I stand. If I am in a position to be able to gain my independence, surely there are agents to help me."

"I am sure you are right, but they won't care about the results as much as I will."

Eve stiffened. Lucy was too much. She was too giving. Eve couldn't trust it. But she needed help. That's why she was there. She was nearly certain she had gotten the proper paperwork out of the house to find the answers she was looking for.

The scholars were going to help her interpret the information. It didn't even matter if they didn't keep her matters private.

Evangeline didn't need to stay in Society, so no matter what they found out, if it was something that would get her ostracized, she didn't even care. But she didn't like the suspicion that the other woman had ulterior motives. She couldn't imagine what they might be, but she couldn't trust her offer of free help out of the goodness of her heart.

Her own family hadn't offered her assistance. Why would this near stranger do so?

Even Mr. Smythe's assistance made a slight bit more sense to her, since she knew he was fascinated with numbers and mathematical mysteries and had shifted his focus to economies, so her situation might be seen in the light of a case study for his scholarly pursuits.

What did Lucy Northcott have to gain?

Evangeline swallowed the questions that wanted to tumble from her mouth even as the young matron clung to her arm and chattered all the way up the stairs. It didn't matter. Eve had something to gain. If the other woman got something from it, she should be glad for it since she didn't think she could pay for the services being offered to her.

Trying to quell her suspicious mind kept her tongue silent, and Lucy continued to fill the air with her cheerful chatter. Eve could barely pay attention but it seemed to be inconsequential until Lucy stopped and looked at her expectantly.

Eve blinked and thought back to what the other woman had been prattling on about. She ought to have tried harder to follow it, but her mind had been bouncing around too much. Between her suspicions about

Lucy and her attraction to Sean and her worries about her future, Evangeline felt torn in too many directions.

But Lucy had asked about Gladys. That was what she was awaiting a response upon.

"It turns out my maid is not an agent for the family, at least not as far as I can tell. And I've been watching closely so I am reasonably certain about my determination."

Lucy laughed at Eve's nervous answer, not bothered by her roundabout explanation, clearly amused by it.

"I do apologize for laughing at you, my dear, but you don't strike me as the sort who isn't usually glib of tongue, so your less than articulate words were amusing."

When Eve waved away her apology, Lucy continued, "Very well, then we will assume likewise. You must have been relieved by that realization," she remarked.

Eve nodded, just realizing the woman was right. She had found comfort in the maid's presence rather than further cause for disquiet. But because she had so much cause for concern, she hadn't even realized that some of it had lessened.

They entered the room without knocking, finding Gladys bent over a trunk, reaching for the last of Eve's things.

"You've been very quick," Eve commended, quickly approaching the wardrobe where the maid had placed her things. "Where have you put the box with the papers?"

"Just here," Gladys responded immediately, indicating a pile that nicely hid the box in question.

"Nicely done," Eve commended once more, glancing back at Lucy before returning her gaze to the maid. "Would you like to be present while we examine the contents or are you too occupied with your responsibilities?"

Eve was glad that she had asked. The maid looked as though she had been offered the most valuable boon.

"You wouldn't mind?" Gladys asked, her face breaking into a wide smile and sparkling eyes.

"Of course not," Eve said immediately. "And it only seems fair since you found most of what we brought."

"Oh no, my lady, I'm sure the file you found will turn out to be most important."

Eve laughed, for a brief moment feeling almost light hearted. "You have just proven my point, though. It is only right that you be there if you wish to be. Or you could be offered a vacation, if you would rather that. I am sure I am perfectly safe her for the time being."

"Oh no, my lady, I would ever so much rather stay here, although I do appreciate the offer. It would be a pleasure to visit me mum, but I would most assuredly enjoy helping with your investigation."

Eve laughed again. "We aren't agents of the crown, but I suppose it is an investigation, isn't it? Very well, bring the box and come along."

Eve didn't bother asking Lucy if it were acceptable to her. From what she could see, the unconventional household should be just fine with the arrangement. They didn't stand on the usual social niceties. And really, it wasn't a social call. It was task oriented. One could argue maids were necessary.

Not that Evangeline was experienced with argument. No one had ever bothered to listen to her long enough for her to express any of her stronger opinions. Maybe that was one more of the things she ought to change in her life. She certainly would if she could gain a home of her own. Even if she couldn't, she would learn to be more firm with Sabina and the rest of the Robertsons.

Eve pushed all unhelpful thoughts from her mind as they hurried back downstairs and joined Mr. Smythe and Roderick Northcott in the library. It was a cleaner looking room than the one Gerald had used. Maybe clean wasn't the right word, she thought as she noticed a bit of dust float by in the sunlight streaming in the window, but she appreciated the lack of clutter.

It was a manly room, but definitely not decorative in any way. It was clear to Evangeline that the room was intended for study.

And that's what they did for the next hour. The papers were distributed between Roderick, Lucy, Gladys, Eve, and Sean as he had insisted she call him.

"If we're going to be so deeply involved in your personal business, surely we shouldn't stand on ceremony, don't you think, lass?" he'd asked her in his thick, pleasant brogue.

"Very well, thank you, Sean," Eve said, cursing the blush that heated her cheekbones.

Quiet settled for a time before Eve's gasp almost echoed through the spacious room.

"What has happened?" Lucy exclaimed almost immediately.

"I, I..." Evangeline couldn't even say the words that were catching at her throat. She stood up clutching the papers in her hand.

Sean approached her urgently, putting his hands on her arms just below her shoulders, and stared into her face with intense concentration.

"Take a deep breath," he ordered her firmly.

Suddenly, all she could see was him and a sudden, irrational urge swept through her to throw herself into his arms. Thankfully his warm, firm grip prevented her from so embarrassing herself.

Hysterical laughter clogged behind the words in her throat, but still a wild grin spread across her face. Finally, another gasp loosened her tongue.

"I think he might have left it all to me."

Sean stared at her even harder before Lucy pushed him out of the way.

“Quit clutching her, Sean. You’re likely to leave bruises and neither of you have even noticed.”

Sean immediately let go and Eve felt the loss before Lucy snatched the papers from her hand, turning her attention away from the riotous sensations coursing through her.

Chapter Thirteen

Sean's hands burned where he had been holding onto the beautiful woman.

He knew from previous conversations with Evangeline that she was level headed and intelligent. If she understood the paperwork said she was her husband's heir, then she was a wealthy woman to be sure.

It was likely set up in a trust, as it was most irregular for a woman to hold properties, but he would have to examine the papers before he knew for certain.

He was intrigued by the thought of advising a wealthy woman.

But he was even more intrigued by the woman before him, wealthy or not. It would be a fascinating task.

He ought to ask his mother to visit. She would know how to set his thoughts straight. The thought helped him regain his equilibrium that had been so set askew by having the lovely woman in his arms. Or rather in his hands. But for the briefest moment he had almost pulled her into his chest.

The urge to hold her for the rest of eternity had been nearly overwhelming. It was most strange. The other scholars would have mocked him mercilessly if they had been there to witness it.

Sean refocused on the matter at hand. The others could rib him later. He had more important things to focus on at the moment. He watched in deepening admiration as Evangeline snatched the papers back from Lucy with a slightly hysterical sounding giggle.

“Those are mine, thank you very much, madam,” she said as she straightened the papers out and laid them on a table where they all could see.

Sean tried to keep his distance but then he found himself leaning over her shoulder to see more clearly. The perfume she must have sprayed in her hair at some point tantalized him along with the sprigs of curls that had escaped the confines of their pins. It took considerable effort to follow her finger where she was pointing out the pertinent points.

“That’s what it means, right? Gerald named me as his successor if something were to happen to him?”

Lucy was obviously not so distracted as he was. She was nodding and clapping her hands.

“You can have all the independence you want, Lady Evangeline,” she pronounced in mock formality, wiggling where she stood.

Evangeline didn’t seem nearly so excited.

“Wouldn’t Ralph have known this? It looks to me as though he signed some of these papers.”

“Why would he have signed them? Since your husband wasn’t nobility, there were no titles or obligation to pass his inheritance to the next male family member like there often are for the aristocracy.” Roderick pointed this out in a tone that was both reasonable and gentle, as though he had no desire to hurt the lady’s feelings.

“But it looks like this is a document informing Ralph. This isn’t the actual document naming me the heir. That must be somewhere else in these papers or perhaps still at the house.”

"Ah, then it would seem your brother-in-law was your husband's heir until you came along."

"That would explain the animosity, then, wouldn't it?"

"I thought you said your husband's family was oddly solicitous of you."

"Now they are, since Gerald's death. But after our marriage, they were rude and dismissive."

"Ah," Roderick said. "Then yes, it would seem that they do know. And have done their best to keep you in the dark, no doubt."

"But why would they be trying to marry me off? I still don't see how that benefits them, especially if everything is mine."

"But you don't know that," Sean said, cutting into the conversation. He cleared his throat. "Or rather, they think you don't know that, and you didn't know. Up until now. And there would be less chance of you finding that out if you are gone. You will have a new family to concern yourself with. They can carry on stealing your wealth if you have remarried."

Roderick watched as Evangeline stared at him, nodding. "That makes a strange sort of sense, I suppose. It seemed to be a challenge for them to be kind to me at first, but now they have grown accustomed to it. Like it's a habit now. But it certainly didn't come naturally. I suppose it's possible it was all a ruse to keep me from asking questions. And I never would have asked, to be honest, except that I have grown weary of their efforts. I never would have thought Gerald would leave everything to me. I just expected there to be a settlement of some sort, that might allow me to find a small cottage somewhere. Who would have thought he would leave everything to me?"

Sean grinned as the woman turned her concentration to the window as though she had to take a moment to contemplate the possibilities. He hoped she still wanted his help.

He was thrilled at the thought of figuring out all the numbers for her. Or with her. He had sufficient respect for her intellect to know she would want to be involved. Just look at her interest in their little investigation.

He was glad for her that she was the one to have found the answer. It might not yet be a complete answer, but it settled for certain that she could gain the independence she sought.

"What if there are more papers changing it?" She suddenly turned back to the room with the question. "I shouldn't get my hopes up too high, should I?"

"Even if that were to be true, we can see your husband was determined to provide for you," Lucy stepped in immediately. "He wouldn't have left you with nothing, even if he changed his heir once more."

"Unless he did it in a fit of pique," Evangeline pointed out.

"Was that in keeping with his temperament?" Roderick asked with a frown.

Rage threatened to flood through Sean when the woman lifted a negligent shoulder as though it were an unimportant matter.

"Pique was in keeping with his temperament but keeping it a secret wasn't. So I suppose you could be right. If he was going to dismiss me from being his heir because he was angry with me, he would ensure I knew all about it." She nodded and smiled. "There is some comfort in that."

Sean snorted.

"There's no comfort to be found in knowing someone is prone to rages, lass," he said firmly. "I know that well."

When the lady's wide, steady gaze threatened to make him spill all his thoughts and feelings, Sean shut the impulse down quickly.

"Shall we continue with the papers? We can know for certain where you stand in that case."

With a firm nod, the woman found a seat and continued her perusal of the sheaf of papers, periodically taking careful notes in a tidy penmanship. Sean could see from where he sat that she would make an excellent scholar. Many ladies, from his limited experience, had such flowy, flowery writing that it was nearly impossible to decipher their meaning.

Like he needed anything more to admire about the woman, Sean thought with a sarcastic lilt.

"He bought the house," Evangeline once again broke the silence, this time in a breathy, shocked tone.

"Did you think it was leased?" Roderick asked, puzzled.

Evangeline waved her hand as though to dismiss his words. "I should rather say that I think he bought a house I admired. If that is the case, and if it turns out to be mine, that solves my dilemma quite nicely. I can just move in there. I could even leave the family to Gerald's house. I have no need of it."

"It could prove to be quite expensive," Sean warned.

"I suppose I ought to amend my words. If we find that I can afford to do so, I would leave the house to the Robertsons. I have no wish to live there, but I have little desire to turn them out."

"Where did they live before your husband passed?" Lucy asked.

"I believe they rented rooms when they were in Town and had a small property near the village where they grew up. Like I mentioned earlier, they didn't take too well to Gerald's marrying me, so we didn't speak much."

"I'm sorry this stirs up difficult sentiments," Roderick said a little stiffly, glancing to his wife for assistance.

Sean never tired of witnessing their partnership. It wasn't something he had seen before. If he could ever find something similar, he would want it for himself, but all the other marriages he had seen appeared quite different.

His mother's was one of the poorest examples. And helping Evangeline demonstrated one more of such. Obviously, her marriage hadn't been terribly happy.

"I beg you pay it no mind," Evangeline said immediately, bringing Sean's thoughts back to the matter at hand. "It is far less difficult to know where one stands. And if he has already bought the house, then I shan't have anything to concern myself with. As long as there are sufficient funds to keep me in gentility, I shall be content. I have no need or desire to live highly or to go about much in Society."

"Won't you grow lonely?" Lucy asked with a frown and a gentle gesture toward her midsection, arousing Sean's suspicions there might be a little one some months hence.

"I can volunteer at some worthy establishment and make friends with my neighbours. And I am certain my brother will still receive me, even if he thinks I've gone soft in the head."

"But will it be enough for you? You must be certain to make sound decisions at this time, Eve," Lucy cautioned. "Don't do anything too hastily."

Evangeline chuckled. "It is kind of you to be concerned. But I have never had much more than I just described. In fact, it sounds absolutely delectable to my thinking."

"Very well, then, let us get down to brass tacks, shall we?" Sean interrupted Lucy's concerned clucking.

He understood his friend's wife was only trying to look out for the lady, but it was turning his stomach to think of anyone trying to match Evangeline up into a Society marriage. It was bad enough she carried a courtesy title.

The rest of the hour passed quickly as everyone was even more focused on the papers they were examining. They were all trying to ascertain if there was any reason to suspect there was paperwork that would supplant what Eve had already found.

Chapter Fourteen

Eve's nausea was threatening to overwhelm her ability to control the urge. She was delighted with what she had found and yet so fearful of putting her trust in it. She didn't want to get her hopes up, but, oh, how high they were already climbing.

She hadn't thought to trust it was possible. Or rather she had hoped there might be a small pittance that would allow her to leave the house Gerald had brought her to and gain her independence from his family.

She would happily rent a room somewhere or a small cottage in a tiny village. Eve had no need to live in high fashion. But to be able to remain in Town would be lovely.

If Gerald *had* provided for her, it would be such a relief. The fact that he had bought the house she had admired told her something. She wasn't sure what, though.

Had he bought it with the intention of gifting it to her at some point? Or had her admiration for it merely brought it to his attention and he'd thought to add it to his collection of properties? Because Eve was fairly certain he had several houses, estates, and properties throughout the realm. Perhaps even beyond the realm.

It was a little overwhelming to think he had left the lot to her.

The family was going to fight her.

That thought terrified her. Part of her wanted to just leave it all to them if it was in fact hers to dispose of as she pleased. But the thought of having such power was seductive, and she thought she might like to try her hand at running Gerald's empire.

He had certainly told her enough throughout the two years she had been married to him to know how he thought on most matters of business, even if he had thought she was too stupid to understand what he was talking about. She could merely make decisions based on what she thought he would do.

Or she could decide for herself.

Everything in her tingled. She could gain her independence and something to occupy herself with all at the same time. She would never again have to turn a gown for lack of funds to order a new one, if what she had read turned out to be truly the final word on the matter.

But the family was definitely going to fight her.

She would need a solicitor. Probably an entire firm of solicitors. Perhaps Mr. Northcott's father could advise her on a successful firm that might consider taking on her business.

Because even if it turned out that she had inherited Gerald's holdings, or rather if she was able to successfully prove it, in order to get control away from the family, she was going to need the assistance of solicitors. No one was going to openly do business with a woman.

Evangeline refused to be disheartened by that thought. It didn't matter. She could have her darling house and do whatever she wished. And if possible, she could run some businesses.

Perhaps Mr. Smythe could be persuaded to leave his scientific pursuits and help her with the mathematics full-time. He could have Gerald's house if he wished. Or one of the other properties.

Ralph and Sabina would want Gerald's house. And Eve would give it to them in an effort to keep peace. Or perhaps to assuage her conscience.

"If your brother-in-law was aware of this development, then they have been robbing you, Eve," Lucy broke their implied, silent agreement not to discuss the matter over supper.

Eve's nausea actually stilled, contrarily enough.

What an odd creature she was turning out to be. Rather than be repulsed by the thought of going into business, she was ecstatic to the point of sickness. And that calmed at the thought of the family stealing from her.

"Well, if that's the case, then I needn't feel guilty about discomfiting them in return, need I?" Eve returned with a grin.

"Not a wit of guilt is to be allowed in this scenario," Lucy answered immediately. "But especially if it is, as I suspect, the case that Mr. Robertson is fully aware of the situation."

"Do you think his wife knows?"

That was Eve's big question.

She had thought the other woman had made a concerted effort to be kind to her, to overcome her initial distress over Gerald's marriage with a young noblewoman. But now, finding out it might have been for mercenary reasons, on the heels of figuring out the woman's push for her to remarry a nobleman was also for selfish reasons, made Eve feel very small and unloved. Even more small and unloved than she had felt most of her life, ever since her mother's death.

Her father had little use for her after Mama's passing. He had only finally taken an interest in her when he had realized he could profit from her existence.

Even her brother hadn't made any effort to dissuade their father from marrying her off to someone he had no desire to socialize with. It made his life far easier.

And with Gerald's death, she was suddenly acceptable once more, and her brother had invited her to move back home. Of course, Eve had been made aware that she could busy herself in the nursery with her young nephew and niece.

It hadn't been difficult to turn down that invitation. But she hadn't really felt welcome in her own marital home, either. As soon as the Robertsons had moved in the day after Gerald's death, it hadn't felt like Eve's home.

Not that it ever really had.

Gerald had been generous with offering to allow her to redecorate, but he had turned up his nose at all of her suggestions so it had really been an empty offer. Perhaps, if he had lived longer, she would have stiffened her backbone and gone ahead with her ideas.

Now, she might never have to consult with anyone again.

She thrilled at the very thought.

"How soon do you think I might move into that house?"

Eve hadn't realized she had voiced her thoughts until she noticed Lucy and her husband exchanging meaningful glances.

Roderick Northcott cleared his throat.

"Let's finish reading through everything you've brought with you first; that will give us a better idea of where you stand. Then we will ask my brother's solicitor to call by and discuss the matter in detail. In the meantime, Sean can start working out some calculations for you as to what sort of finances you will need to establish yourself. That information will be helpful if you want to make an offer to the Robertsons rather than making it a legal matter."

Eve watched with a degree of envy as Mr. Northcott exchanged another expressive glance with his wife. It was as though the two of them could have entire conversations without saying a word.

She had never had that with Gerald. Eve wouldn't allow her gaze to search for Sean's eyes. She had no interest in silent conversations with anyone, she insisted to herself.

Roderick continued. "You could have criminal charges brought against the Robertsons if it does turn out that they knew. So, you will have to decide if the potential for scandal is worth it to you."

"No," Eve answered immediately, not needing to give the matter any thought. "I cannot be happy with what they did, if they did indeed do it, but he is Gerald's brother. I cannot turn him into a criminal. Or rather, I suppose, if it's true, he did that to himself, but I wouldn't want to make it known. Both for my own sake and for my nephews."

Her heart clutched. "Even if the boys knew, they are misguided boys. I don't want to have any part in ruining their lives."

"They were making an effort to ruin yours," Lucy pointed out. Eve couldn't argue with her reasoning.

"Perhaps. But they probably didn't think of it in those terms. We will never be able to really know what they were thinking. Whatever the case, there is likely to be some sort of scandal if I'm not very careful or if they refuse to accept the truth of matters. Or, perhaps no one will even notice. It isn't as though Ralph or Sabina are invited anywhere. They were hoping I would arrange it. Now there is no question of that."

"We will make sure no scandal attaches itself to you; you can be sure of that." Lucy's tone was firm and determined.

"How could you possibly ensure that?" Eve wasn't being rude by asking the question, she just couldn't fathom how Lucy thought to make such a guarantee.

"I don't intend to brag, but Roderick's family is rather well connected."

"And our friends are even more so," Roderick added.

"Or you could just renounce Society and be done with it," Sean interjected while the other gentlemen at the table chuckled.

"Smythe doesn't care too much for our noble peers," Ellis Dorval, Viscount Severn, the chemist, told her, as though she hadn't already figured that out from the way the man's lip curled whenever anyone with a title was mentioned.

"You should have seen him at school with all the little titled urchins. It took all his effort not to knock their heads together," Pierce Darby, the astronomer said with a laugh

"You were one of those urchins," the viscount reminded his friend.

"No, I wasn't," the man protested. "I don't even have a title now, unlike some of us."

"There's nothing inherently wrong with a title," the viscount protested in a tone that told Eve this conversation had been worn many times.

"Sure there is, since there's nothing done to earn it," Sean said and Mr. Darby nodded in agreement

"There was at some point in time. And it's a demonstration of loyalty," Viscount Severn said in an aggrieved but calm tone.

Sean snorted. Eve couldn't blame him. Titles were silly for the most part. But it was what she knew. She wasn't so revolutionary that she intended to renounce hers. Even if she were put beyond the pale by taking up business.

She would retain her title for whatever it might be worth. Even if it was only a courtesy.

“What makes you so adamantly opposed to titles, Mr. Smythe? And why would you be in association with such ones as these if this is how you truly feel?” Eve didn’t mean to put him on the spot, but it seemed to her that he was being rather daft.

“His father is a titled bloke,” one of his friends answered when it appeared he had no intention of doing so.

Eve wasn’t certain what she ought to say in reply. It was not what she had been expecting. Heat flooded her face, and she knew she was blushing.

“I wasn’t illegitimate, if that’s what you’re thinking,” Sean exclaimed.

“You needn’t blush like a schoolgirl. And you ought to keep a civil tongue in your head,” he added in an aside to his friend. Or at least his fellow scholar. Eve wasn’t so sure that they were friends from the way they spoke with one another from time to time.

“Perhaps this is a conversation for the parlour, not the dining room,” Lucy said as she stood. “We can have our port and tea there and let the kitchen staff finish for the day.”

With a nod to the servant standing by the door, Lucy ended the argument and led the way from the room. Eve couldn’t help but admire the other woman’s determined character.

Chapter Fifteen

Sean knew he should have avoided the topic. Even more he should have known the others wouldn't have been able to prevent themselves from ribbing him. And now he was going to have to tell this seemingly fragile woman about his scandalous childhood.

Could childhoods be scandalous?

His certainly had been, but it ought to be a given that it wasn't possible. Children obviously had no control over their pasts. It shouldn't be possible for there to be scandal attached to it.

But there you had it. There was nothing just in the world. Especially not the world of the English aristocracy.

How his father had been able to divorce his mother and marry another with nary a breath of censure toward him never ceased to amaze Sean. The man appeared to be impossible to defeat or embarrass. Even as he persisted in trying to re-establish a relationship with Sean. Every time Sean rejected the man's overtures it only seemed to disappoint him, but never made him give up.

But the man also had his blue-blooded little heirs that he had wanted. With his wealthy, blue-blooded wife. Not to say she was royalty, but as the daughter of a marquis, she was the next thing to it.

Of course, the old man wanted Sean's forgiveness now that he was nearing his grave. Sean's grandfather and father both thought he ought to forget how they had treated him and his mother. But no five-year-old boy should ever be treated like that. To have his rightful place snatched from him because a better opportunity presented itself was sinful.

Not that Sean had any interest in being a part of that man's lineage.

Sean's mum had been good enough for the younger son but as soon as Sean's dad had become his father's heir upon the death of his grandfather and brother, his entire bearing had changed. He had become mean, cruel, and filled with hate toward everything about their life in Scotland. Finally, he had travelled back to his home in England and never returned, only sending a messenger to inform them that they were no longer his family. He had arranged an annulment.

Young Sean hadn't known what that meant nor understood why he and his mother were suddenly outcasts. He also couldn't understand how the seemingly perfectly binding marriage his parents had entered into could suddenly be dissolved without a by your leave.

He still couldn't understand that one. And it was one of the main reasons he hated the English. How could their system allow for illegitimating a child and his young mum who had never done anything wrong in her life?

That and the fact that his wicked father was English.

While the logical part of his brain told him he shouldn't paint everyone with the same brush, the fact that his father and now his young half siblings were readily accepted everywhere in *tonnish* Society while he was still often treated as an outcast, told him all he needed to know about the English standards and morals.

"Viscount Sutton is my father," he finally blurted out when everyone was seated and low murmurs of conversation were resuming in the casual room.

Lady Evangeline's frown demonstrated her confusion.

"Aren't you older than Francis?" she asked, referring to the viscount's son and heir, one of the half siblings Sean had not grown up with.

She had blushed earlier when it had been mentioned and then he had claimed being legitimate. Sean knew he was so in the eyes of God but not those of man. Even the Scottish and English churches were different. And well they should be, Sean thought. The English were heathens. That thought bolstered his flagging spirits.

"I am so, by several years. Six or eight, I think. I don't rightly know when the boy was born."

Her tight but polite smile actually warmed him. She obviously knew there were details she didn't understand but didn't intend to press him about it. She also wasn't judging him as most in her position would.

"My father spent all of my mother's reportedly generous dowry on drink and loose living after my mother died. That's why there was nearly nothing left of the estate when my brother was coming of age to marry and how they hatched the plan of wedding me off to Gerald."

It wasn't news but it was an interesting demonstration of her compassion. She didn't understand what exactly Sean was trying to tell her, but she was expressing her own experience with unkind family.

Despite being English, she had a heart. Just like Roddie and Lucy. And even some of the other gents, despite their constant ribbing and needling.

It was possible the English as a nation weren't the spawn of the devil. Was it just his father, then? The sudden thought felt like treachery.

That idea would take some getting used to. Sean wasn't sure if it was worth it. He still had no intention of taking part in High Society.

But then, neither did the rest of them. He settled back with his glass and a smile. The conversation started to revolve around Pierce's discovery of the day. Sean had nothing to add. He hadn't invented any new equations since soon after making Evangeline's acquaintance. Perhaps his brain had turned to the mush he suspected.

But when Evangeline smiled gently in his direction, he couldn't even be angry about it.

Was losing your intellect over a woman worth it? He was determined to find out.

But first he had to help the widow figure out how much money she needed to live in a reasonable style. And then, he needed to help her manage extreme amounts of money if the paperwork she'd found proved to be true. There were enough calculations needed that he could forget his wretched father's family.

If only his so-called cousin would stop writing to him.

But Sean couldn't think about Carrick and his blasted letters right now. He had numbers to sort out. And feelings to avoid. Thinking about Viscount Harlow was only going to stir up more of those. But mathematics could be counted on, not something that could be said about anything related to his father or that man's family.

It didn't matter, it couldn't matter, how often Carrick wrote to him asking for an audience, begging really, but that didn't matter, Sean insisted again. There were numbers to sort.

And sort they did.

Sean would escape from the breakfast room each day, returning to his shed, thinking he needed a break from the others, but then he would miss Lady E and her inquiring mind. There was nothing he enjoyed more than showing her how to calculate compounding interest or how a mortgage rate worked.

Her intellect would rival that of the other scholars. Sean could hardly believe how quickly she caught on to anything he was showing her.

But then she found the oddest document amongst the others she had brought, and the entire household lost their collective minds for a time. They thought there was to be a treasure hunt.

Sean was already bent over the papers they'd spread across the table, his brow furrowed in concentration. "These numerical sequences..." he muttered. "They're not like any financial records I've seen."

"Perhaps because they're not meant to be financial," Pierce Darby said from the doorway.

He strode in, brandishing one of the papers Eve had found between the Alexandria books. "Look at these coordinates. They follow an ancient mapping system. And these poetic riddles..."

He broke off, glancing at Eve. "Begging your pardon, my lady. We shouldn't get distracted from your inheritance matters."

"No, please," Eve found herself saying. "What do you make of them?"

"Well," Pierce's eyes lit up, "the references to 'knowledge lies' and 'wisdom's keep' - combined with Gerald's collection of books about Alexandria..."

"Not this again," Ellis groaned good-naturedly. "Not every old paper leads to lost libraries."

"Let's focus on the settlement papers first," Roderick suggested firmly. But Eve noticed Sean slipping the mysterious documents aside rather than dismissing them entirely. There would be time to unravel Gerald's other secrets later.

“What do you think it is?” one of the scholars asked, Sean thought it was Lincoln but he couldn’t be sure.

“Surely it’s a pile of gold,” another chortled.

“Don’t be daft, it has to be a library or a lost work, didn’t you see the clue?” This from the baron who stopped by for a visit with some of his school chums. None of them respected his intellect, though, so they didn’t take his opinion to carry much weight.

Eve had just laughed as everyone discussed and squabbled over the pertinent papers.

“I’m fairly certain I’ve already found my treasure, gentlemen,” she said in her gentle voice at supper that night. “I didn’t think Gerald was so fanciful as to believe in lost treasures, and I cannot guarantee there is any veracity to that old document, but you are welcome to it, if any of you wish to pursue it.”

Sean shook his head. She was far too generous. What if she did need funds after this was all said and done? He took her to task over the matter the next day.

“You know there isn’t a guarantee of anything until you have the money firmly settled in an account with your name on it, don’t you?” Sean asked her in a firm tone as they left the breakfast room.

“Of course,” she replied immediately with a crease in her forehead, seemingly not understanding where he was going with this question. “We’ve talked of little else in between calculations. All the calculations in the world aren’t going to do me much good if Ralph can produce documents that supplant mine.”

“That’s just it, Evie,” Sean pointed out. “You shouldn’t have given the fellows your other treasure documents until you know for certain where you stand.”

That had prompted one of her light, tinkling laughs.

"Sean, really?" she asked as she got some of her laughter under control. "You cannot truly tell me you believe in that nonsense, do you?"

"It was in with all the other papers," Sean said in what he thought was a reasonable tone that only set her off laughing again.

"We cannot say for certain where those ones came from. Gladys and I were skulking about the house for days hiding our actions from the Robertsons. They might have been from some fanciful work of fiction for all we know and just got mixed in with everything else when Gladys was hiding it in the trunk."

"But you don't know that it isn't real, either."

"No, I suppose I don't," Eve returned. "But I won't have the time to chase after other treasures if I'm running a shipping company along with a mining company and a trading house and a bank, now will I?"

Sean grinned at her.

"I do hope you didn't want to chase along with the others because if you're truly going to help me, you won't have the time for that either."

Sean shook his head firmly. "I can't see there being much need for a mathematician in a treasure hunt anyhow. They need the cartographer, but he isn't due back for a while."

They continued on with her education in economics after that, but it wasn't helping Sean keep his heart out of her hands.

Chapter Sixteen

The week with the Northcotts and their scholars flew by. Evangeline wished the time would slow. They were now nearly completely sure that she was the sole heir of Gerald's vast fortune. And it was decidedly vast and deep.

It was actually a challenge for Eve to grasp the extent of her newfound wealth. The only possible change would be if Ralph and Sabina could produce a credible, more recent, document that would possibly replace the paperwork she had found.

But knowing Gerald the way that she did, Evangeline couldn't believe that he would have done so without telling her about it. There hadn't been any quarrels between them that would have resulted in his being angry enough to disinherit her after having already made so many arrangements to provide well for her upon his death.

Even the fact that he had bought the house she had admired spoke volumes about his intentions. Evangeline wondered if he had somehow suspected he might not live long and hadn't bothered to tell her.

She would never know for certain.

What she did know is the man had respected her more than she had realized. Or at least far more than he did his own family. That bolstered her confidence in her ability to manage all the responsibilities that were going to come upon her when it all became known.

"You will have to return to Town," Lucy finally pronounced after everything had been examined and compiled and Sean was busily making various calculations. "There's a rout tomorrow night, I'm sure we've all been invited to it. You ought to go."

"I would rather stay here with you a while longer." Eve was nearly overwhelmed with anxiety over the thought of returning to Town and facing the Robertsons.

"You are always welcome here," Lucy said immediately. "But you ought to get on with organizing yourself and your future. That is why you came to us," she concluded almost gently, obviously trying to curb her controlling ways.

Evangeline nodded. "You are right. But I am not afraid to admit that I am afraid."

She laughed a little over her own words.

"You shan't go alone. We'll all go with you." Lucy paused before amending her statement. "Well, maybe not all the men. But Roderick, Sean, and I will certainly accompany you. Roderick and his brother or father will help with the lawyers, and Sean will do the calculations. You and I will make the rounds and perhaps do some shopping. You could even attend whichever event your sister-in-law has selected for you. That could be highly entertaining."

Eve tried hard not to starch up over Lucy's statement. Lucy was her friend. Lucy had been kind and welcoming to her even before this visit. She had taken Eve and her maid into her home and helped her discover some of her own strengths and dreams for the future.

Eve shouldn't take offence over one statement. But she couldn't leave it be.

"Entertaining for who?" she asked, trying not to sound belligerent but unsure if she had succeeded.

Sean's snort of laughter let her know he was aware something was amiss. Even Roderick had straightened in his seat. Eve thought he might have moved incrementally closer to his wife as though to offer his protection. Eve's irritation clenched tighter.

But Lucy didn't bristle in return. She actually burst into laughter.

"Well, it will certainly be entertaining for me, to be sure. But I would hope for you as well."

Lucy's laughter died and her brow furrowed and then she hurried over to Evangeline's seat, dropping to her knees before the lady and clasping her hand.

"Do say you haven't been hurt by my senseless words, my dear friend. I meant nothing foul by them, I promise you. But you really must strive to see the humour in this, as in all things. Else you will be a drudge forever. Don't you think it will be a lark to take over Gerald's businesses?"

"I do," Eve answered in a cautious tone, noticing that Sean was inching closer to her, as though he were ready to champion her cause if need be.

"There, you see? And everything connected to that should be diverting for you, as well. Including putting the family's collective nose out of joint for what they attempted to do to you. Even if you end up making a large settlement upon them just to smooth the way, you will surely have much to occupy yourself with once everything is transferred to your name. And you'll have that lovely house you want. It shall all be perfectly pleasing and you are to delight in it all."

Eve couldn't resist Lucy's enthusiasm. She too started to laugh.

"Very well, Lucy, you are right. I shall choose to be entertained by the process rather than worrying myself sick about it. And if you come and remain by my side, surely it will have to be diverting. It can be nothing but delightful."

"That's the spirit," Lucy crowed even as Roderick interjected.

"Lucy cannot remain by your side throughout the entire process, though, my lady," he pointed out.

"No, I don't suppose she can," Eve agreed right away despite her reluctance.

"But we shall be with you for a time, I promise you. We'll even come to your dreadful house to assist you with choosing what to take with you into your new life."

"But you shan't lift a finger," Roderick warned.

Evangeline narrowed her eyes at her hosts.

"What are you not telling me? Have I been far too preoccupied with my own affairs that I have missed something terribly obvious?" Eve's eyes widened with shock. "Are you increasing?"

Delight and horror warred within her. Eve refused to be jealous. She was just learning how to have friends. She couldn't ruin it by not being happy for them. But her refusal of jealousy didn't actually make it real.

Lucy's hand hovered over her midsection while she smiled and nodded happily. "But it's still very new, that's why I didn't say anything before, and it shan't interfere with our plans. Although it is one of the reasons why I'd be delighted to come to Town and shop with you."

Eve smiled and nodded, feeling in a little bit of a daze after that revelation. Lucy was right, she needed to get back to Town and get her own affairs sorted out.

She couldn't rely on the Northcotts to do everything for her, not even their scholars. Sean was lovely and had helped her considerably, but Evangeline was once more reminded that she could only rely upon herself.

Gratitude for what the Scholarly Society had done for her warred with her jealousy and sense of insecurity. Eve was a maelstrom of conflicting feelings she tried her best to hide.

"You shouldn't put yourself out for me, Lucy. You have done enough. And in your state, you must have a care," she finally stammered out. "And I shouldn't take more of your time than I have already. I will leave for Town in the morning. Perhaps Gladys and I should even leave right now. It isn't so very far back to Town."

Nothing Lucy and the others said could dissuade her so all they did was promise to follow in her wake.

"Have a care, Lucy. You are right, I will attend the rout, but you needn't follow so closely. You need your strength."

Eve tried to convince Lucy not to exert herself, but the woman was adamant.

After that, she was quick to pack up her things, collect her maid, and be on her way back to London. Of course, she waited until early the next day to actually take her leave. She would rather die a thousand deaths than have it appear that she was running craven.

Even if she was.

It was the work of a coward to be jealous of a friend. But there was little she could do about her wretched feelings.

There was a riot of conflicting emotions warring within her when Eve followed Gladys into the carriage and settled her skirts. She lifted her eyebrows in haughty inquiry when she realized her maid was staring at her.

"What happened, m'lady?" Gladys asked once they were on the road, well away from anyone who might overhear.

"Nothing happened, Gladys. It's just time to go home. We had done all we could do at the Scholarly estate."

Gladys made a noncommittal murmur in her throat, obviously not believing Eve's explanation. "I understood we were to stay for the full seven days despite your having as much done as could be done from there."

"It was decided that was being cowardly."

"Decided by whom?"

"Are you being impertinent?" Eve asked with a glimmer of amusement.

"Not intentionally," Gladys answered with a hint of answering laughter.

"Don't you think I ought to get on with things? Shouldn't I confront the Robertsons and find out exactly where I stand?"

"I do, but I don't think you ought to do it alone. Shouldn't you have a team or crew or however you'd like to name it, friends or partners who will watch out for you as you navigate this next stage?"

"I don't have any of those." Eve stated baldly before a smile softened her. "Other than you, of course. I shall be counting on your support quite immensely."

"And you'll have it, to be sure, m'lady. And the other servants, too, of course. But there's only so much someone in service can do. You would have done well to allow the Northcotts and their scholars to lend you countenance."

The maid frowned. "I appreciate your declaration of friendship, my lady, but you know all those fine folks stood as your friends as well.

"I believe I have sufficient countenance for my own needs," Eve countered firmly, refusing the guilt that threatened to swamp her.

She was being foolish and couldn't seem to stop herself. But then she relented. "I expect they will follow on the morrow. I just chose not to travel up to Town with them. There was no need for us to wait. We can get home, get rested from the travels, and start on any arrangements."

"But will you confront the family on your own?"

"No, I will wait until I have spoken with a solicitor. I might be having a tiff but I'm not daft."

Gladys snorted with her effort to contain her laughter. "My lady, you are a complete card."

Evangeline grinned. She had never considered herself the least bit amusing. But she liked the idea. And she loved the idea of her new, independent life that was just on the horizon. Provided she didn't let it slip through her fingers.

That was what she worried about the most. What if the family fought her? Surely they would. Would they take her to court? Could they win if they did so?

She needed a strong team of solicitors at her back. Gladys wasn't wrong in that regard. Eve might not feel as though she could depend on family or friends, but she did need a team to help her accomplish her aims.

It wasn't the same as relying on people when you had hired them. That was the sort of relationship you could trust. If you were paying for their services, you could rely on the fact that they would be accomplished.

Yes, she was cynical, but Eve didn't care. It would protect her feelings. She had learned that the hard way. She didn't need to learn that lesson again.

But she would accept the Northcotts' help, at least in so far as hiring the solicitors. And perhaps their countenance for the next week or two. She wouldn't presume any further than that, especially not with Lucy in a delicate condition.

She didn't wish to be selfish about it. But if Eve were seen to be in the folds of Roderick's family, she knew that would go a long way to protecting her reputation if Ralph and Sabina tried to make trouble for her.

They were sure to try. Why wouldn't they?

Evangeline was about to take away what they had tried to steal from her. Eve didn't feel guilty about that, but she did have some qualms about the process of how to accomplish it.

Sabina knew her well. She would know how to hurt her. If Eve allowed it. Which she wouldn't. Or at least she would make every effort not to allow the other woman to hurt her.

Evangeline had a backbone. She fully intended to exert it. So perhaps Sabina didn't actually know her at all.

A small smile stuck itself to her face as they pulled to a stop in front of the house and a servant rushed out to hold the door for her.

"Welcome home, my lady," the footman said with what appeared to be a genuine smile and relief on his face. Eve tried not to frown over it.

"Is all well here, John?" she asked quietly as Gladys descended from the carriage behind her.

"I cannot say, my lady."

That was an answer in itself. Anxiety threatened. But Evangeline lifted her chin.

Whether or not she was the heir, this was still her home. She had a right to be there. And if she was the heir as they had discovered, then she had the right to ensure no one else was. Squaring her shoulders after nodding at the footman, Eve marched into the house.

"You're home earlier than expected," Sabina called from the doorway of Eve's bedroom, which had been left open to allow the coming and going of the footmen with her baggage. "It wasn't to your taste, was it?"

"I actually had a lovely time, thank you. But I did miss Town far more than I could have thought possible.

There is a rout this evening and a play at the theatre later this week I'd like to attend."

"How did you even know about your invitations?" Sabina frowned, confirming some of Evangeline's suspicions.

"The invitation to the rout arrived before I left," Eve answered dismissively.

"Would you take me with you?"

"Do you think you'd be comfortable in that crowd?" She asked the question gently, not wishing to be deliberately hurtful.

Eve still didn't think she could be intentionally rude or cruel to the other woman even if Sabina had knowingly worked against her. There was an urge to do so, but that was spite or pique. And Eve truly didn't think she could actually do it even if she wanted to.

"Why wouldn't I be comfortable?"

"Well, you shan't know anyone, for one thing."

"I'll know the wives of the bank's clients."

"They will be the least receptive to your approach, I can assure you. The gentry would prefer to think money doesn't exist, except in copious amounts that can be whispered about. Ladies will not welcome you if you intend to allude to that relationship."

Sabina frowned and looked as though she were about to protest.

"I could ask the hostess if I can bring you if you're sure you'd like to attend. My invitation was only for me, so I cannot just show up with someone else. But I will ask for you."

Sabina opened her mouth but then closed it once more. It was clear to Evangeline she hadn't realized the complexities.

"You're right. It would be better to wait for an invitation. Perhaps I could make calls with you one day, now that you seem more ready to go about in Society."

"That's probably a better idea. Then an invitation is much more likely."

Eve still didn't think Sabina was going to ever be welcomed into Society even if there wasn't the question of Evangeline's inheritance. But it was a more likely possibility if she had actually been introduced to any of the usual hostesses.

"Are you really feeling up to going out after you've been travelling all day?"

"The country was remarkably restorative," Eve answered.

"It would seem so," Sabina sniffed. "You seem like a different person."

"Grieving takes a lot out of one," Eve said softly.

"And are you finished?" Sabina's tone turned harsh.

"No, but I think the initial shock is finally past. No one could have possibly thought Gerald would be taken from us so soon. I thought he was as healthy as an ox."

Sabina almost smiled at Eve's simile but sniffed with censure instead.

"There was always some concern about his heart," Sabina finally said, nearly shocking Eve to her toes.

"He never said a word of it to me," Eve argued.

"He wouldn't have wanted to admit to a weakness to his young and beautiful new bride, now, would he?"

What was Evangeline to say to that? There wasn't much she could do or say, so she just turned back to her unpacking.

Sabina had often in the past year, since she and Ralph had moved in, insisted they were family. Eve didn't think she needed to stand on ceremony with family. Sabina had come to her room. She could entertain herself if she wished to stay.

After a strained, silent moment, Sabina must have realized Evangeline wasn't going to drop everything in order to cater to her as she had been inclined to do previously. With a sniff, she left the room without another word.

"She was right, m'lady," Gladys said quietly from where she was shaking out a gown by the wardrobe. "You have changed."

"Everyone changes, Gladys," Eve countered, feeling a little flustered by the observation, not wanting to examine the feelings that might have resulted in the change.

"Perhaps, but you hadn't seemed to in the last couple of years. Not like you have in the last few days." There was a brief pause before Gladys hurried to add. "That was not meant as any sort of criticism, my lady. Far from it. I'm not sure what Sabina's thoughts are, but I think it's delightful that you seem to have grown more confident or something. It is fitting. That's the right word for it."

"Thank you," Eve felt flattered and bolstered by the maid's words. "I do appreciate that. And I appreciate your help in achieving that state. I never would have managed on my own."

"Sure you would have, eventually," Gladys argued faithfully.

Eve smiled her gratitude but shook her head a little. Maybe in a long eventuality. But then, would there have been anything to discover? Or would she have finally gained her independent spirit only to find out there was no means of following through?

How dreadful it would be to feel full of desire to live on her own only to have to move in with her brother's family. How he would crow about that.

Now, with her head held high, Eve knew she would be able to have her own home and make her own decisions. Even if she had to concede much of Gerald's holdings to Ralph, Eve was confident they would be able to retain enough for her to be sufficiently comfortable.

Sean was fully confident they would be able to manage even better than that.

Thoughts of Sean sent a flutter through her midsection. Eve didn't want to think about what the flutter might mean. Just because they seemed to have much in common didn't mean she wanted to throw all her lovely new independence away.

He was handsome, intelligent, and seemed very kind. At least when he could forget she was English, she thought with amusement even as her heart twisted for the little boy who had been so rejected by his ignoble father.

What a ridiculous misuse of the word nobility. It ought never have been applied to someone's birth rights. Just being born to a titled man did not make one noble, that was clearly evident by both their fathers' actions.

Sabina would disapprove of Sean, just as much as he would disapprove of her. Eve could barely imagine their meeting. But it would be amusing if it would ever happen. Maybe she could arrange it. If she were seen in the company of the Northcotts, that would increase her popularity. Hostesses would be inclined to include Sabina if they thought it would please Evangeline.

Eve sighed. It wouldn't really please her. She didn't think it would be a kindness to the other woman even if Sabina thought it was according to her wishes.

Lucy was right, though. The Robertsons had treated her abominably. She didn't owe them her loyalty. Gerald wouldn't have expected it of her, she was sure.

It didn't take long to prepare for the rout. She was far more eager than she had ever been to attend a Society event. She could only hope the Northcotts got there in time. Never mind that she had run away from them like a scalded cat.

She was counting on their presence.

Chapter Seventeen

"Well that was odd," Lucy remarked quietly as they stood in the doorway watching the carriage drive away. "Was it something someone said? Did any of the gentlemen make her uncomfortable do you suppose?"

As Roderick escorted his wife away making suitably soothing noises, Sean didn't bother telling them he suspected it was the coming bairn that might have made the lady uncomfortable. Or rather the young woman's conflicted feelings might have discomfited her.

He had been studying her for days and even though Evangeline had made every effort to conceal her shifting emotions, Sean was reasonably sure he had learned to read her expressions.

"Are we still going to meet her in Town?" he called out to the Northcotts' retreating backs, not willing to abandon the plan despite how she had run away.

"Of course," Lucy called down the stairs, not bothering to turn around. "Some of us can behave rationally."

Sean chuckled, knowing she was referring to herself but not agreeing with her assessment.

He looked forward to seeing Evangeline in her natural setting. It was likely to dampen the feelings that brewed within him. He would still help her with her mathematics and financial equations, but he welcomed the dispensation of his complicated feelings. Seeing her with the English *ton* should do the job nicely.

Mathematicians didn't need feelings. They shouldn't even have them. That was the whole point. Numbers were dependable. They always did what they were supposed to do. They never let you down.

Now he was sounding like a five-year-old. Sean was sufficiently versed in matters of the mind to know where his feelings stemmed from and why the whining voice in his head was five years old. But he wasn't the daft scholar studying those inner workings nor was he terribly interested in them.

Numbers would keep him company.

But for tonight, he was going to Town.

It should have felt long and boring but before any of them knew it, they were being welcomed by their hostess and drifting through the rooms. Sean told himself he wasn't searching for Evangeline but even as he did so he knew he was lying.

To his shock, he found her in a quiet but obviously heated discussion with another woman.

"Are you well?" It was like a compulsion, he had to intervene.

"Oh, Sean, are you here?" she asked him, blinking as though confused. The urge to pull her into his arms and comfort her was ridiculously strong.

"Who is this, Evangeline?" the ugly woman Eve had been arguing with asked in a snide tone.

Before his eyes, Eve transformed. Gone was the confusion and even the ire.

Suddenly she was the ice maiden who had shown up at the estate two weeks prior. A polite smile barely moved her lips.

"Sabina, allow me to introduce Mr. Sean Smythe. He is one of the scholarly gentlemen who works with my friend's husband."

So this was her sister-in-law. The one pushing Evangeline toward a nobleman, any nobleman, it would seem.

The calculating woman's eyes narrowed to beads as she stared at him with obvious disapproval. For a brief moment he saw amusement gleam in Eve's expression, but she blinked it away.

"Was it to meet him that you insisted on attending this evening?" Sabina hissed.

"I wasn't privy to the guest list." Eve's tone was one of controlled ire. "Including your name, I might add. I wonder why you asked me to bring you if you already had an invitation of your own."

Suddenly Eve must have noticed Lucy by the door as her face softened slightly and she lifted a hand in greeting. "I do hope whoever sponsored you will make you comfortable, Sabina. I have a friend I need to speak with."

Without another word, she turned away from the obviously angry woman. Sean wasn't sure what he ought to do. Eve hadn't included him in her farewell, such that it was. But he didn't want to appear to be chasing after her, so he remained where he was.

"And how did you get in here?" Sabina asked rudely. Sean thought he might ask her the same, but he didn't so lower himself.

"I was included in the invitation my sponsors received."

Sabina sniffed as though she disapproved of his answer and it took all Sean's will to control the urge to laugh.

"Have you enjoyed any of the entertainments yet this evening, Mrs. Robertson? I heard there is some lively music in one of the withdrawing rooms."

"I haven't yet had an opportunity to visit the various rooms," she answered stiffly.

Sean wished he could question her further but didn't want to cause any sort of stir.

"You need to stay away from Lady Evangeline."

To his shock the older woman hurled the words at him in a vehement hiss. He didn't think anyone around them had heard her, but it couldn't be hidden that she was clearly taking him to task over something. Before he could think of anything to say in reply, she had stalked away from him.

It would have been highly amusing if not for the fact that the older woman was still a connection of Lady Evangeline, besides the other tricky fact that he and his friends were about to stir up even more trouble for the strange woman and her family. Better not to draw any more attention than necessary to them now.

But what was he to say or do about the woman's words? Should he tell Evangeline what had been said? Or Lucy and Roderick? They would know what to do.

Or perhaps he ought to just keep silent. He would decide after he saw how the evening progressed.

Sean forced himself to wander through the rooms. He was well skilled at socializing even if he found nearly all Society events deadly dull. This one wasn't the worst he had attended.

There were genuinely interesting individuals present. The sort you could talk to about something more stimulating than the weather or the latest tidbit of gossip.

Sean couldn't care less about who had become engaged or which gentleman had most recently lost his fortune at a gaming table, so he didn't want to hear about those sorts of things. But who was investing in new rail ties or who had found ore on their land might be interesting.

Sean suspected those things would be of immense interest to some of the other fellows at the institute. And Roderick would likely wish to invest in some of those matters. He delved a little deeper before he turned his attention back to what might be happening with Lady Evangeline.

It didn't take him long to find her. Once again, she was in the company of her sister-in-law, Mrs. Robertson. And she looked just as unhappy about it as the last time he had found them together.

Not that anyone else was likely to be aware of that fact.

The woman held herself together very well. It was a scholarly quality, in Sean's opinion. He did appreciate that he could tell that she was uncomfortable, though. It made him feel as though he shared a secret with the beautiful woman.

It appeared to Sean as though she were trying to politely extricate herself from an uncomfortable situation. Sabina didn't appear to be allowing Eve to leave the conversation.

Baron Heath, the gentleman they were with, looked slightly confused but determined to stand his ground. Sean had to admire that determination even if he didn't like it.

Then Mrs. Robertson was beckoning to another gentleman and Sean watched in fascination as an expression of mortification spread across Evangeline's face before quickly being replaced with her polite façade. Sean fixed his gaze upon the gentleman approaching.

His stomach lurched when he saw that it was his cousin. Distant half cousin, but a blood relative through his dastard of a father.

It was Carrick, Viscount Harlow. In Sean's opinion the man was as much of a louse as Sean's father. And not just because he was an Englishman.

Sean didn't make a habit of knowing very much about his father's relations, but he had ears in his head and hadn't been able to avoid hearing about the various misdeeds of the Harlows. They were old tales, at least in connection with Harlow, but still, Sean didn't think a bird could change its plumage.

Really, Sean should be grateful he hadn't grown up with his father or that man's family. They surely would have been a terrible influence upon him. They weren't to be trusted, that was certain.

It irked Sean that similar blood ran in his own veins. His mother would be mortified to know he was at the same social event as ones such as they.

Evangeline didn't look very pleased by it either. But she smiled and nodded, shaking hands with the charlatan as though he had a right to touch her. Sean's hands tightened into fists but he quickly shoved them behind his back. He couldn't shame Roderick and Lucy or Evangeline by causing a scene no matter how satisfying it might be for him.

But he didn't stop watching the scenario play out before him.

He was fascinated to watch Eve quickly but politely put an end to the conversation. It was obvious Sabina didn't have the experience Eve did to hide her true feelings. The other woman was clearly livid over Eve's termination of the interaction.

Sean sidled closer in order to hear what was said.

"Why are you being so churlish, Evangeline? You know we would benefit from this." Sabina's hiss carried more than she realized.

"You might, but I wouldn't," Eve countered, turning back to her sister-in-law and speaking quietly. "I've told you, Sabina, I have no interest in remarrying, especially not to someone of your choosing. I am an independent woman now. If I ever chose to wed again, it would be my choice, not yours or anyone else's. Surely you can understand that after my father arranged my marriage with Gerald."

"Didn't that work out for your good?" Sabina demanded with a cruel twist of her lips.

"This isn't up for discussion, Sabina." Eve appeared determined to keep the other woman at arm's length but still trying not to cause a scene.

To Sean's shock, as he was watching, Mrs. Robertson's gaze fixed upon him. "It's him, isn't it? You have become stubborn because of another man."

The woman was obviously a clunch. Or perhaps she was soused. In either case she was becoming shrill, and Evangeline looked as though she were about to expire from embarrassment.

"Don't be more foolish than necessary, Sabina. You shouldn't be here, and you are about to make a scene. I will not stand for it."

"You have no say over me," Sabina said with a curl of her lip before tacking on a sarcastic, "my lady. We can have you out on your ear without a by your leave if you cross us," she added in a hard tone.

"We'll just see about that," Evangeline said before she turned on her heel and left the other woman gaping after her.

Chapter Eighteen

"Have you been able to find me a solicitor?" Evangeline asked Roderick in a low tone as soon as she was close enough to ask without drawing attention.

Heat filled her cheeks when she realized she was being rude. "My apologies. I ought to have asked how your drive up to Town went and if all is well with Lucy."

"Lucy is as delightful as ever, and you never have to stand on ceremony with me or with any of us. She was a bit fagged from the drive so she has already made her excuses to our hostess and returned to Everleigh House. But she ordered me to remain and ensure you were well and to give you the message that yes, indeed, my father has arranged an appointment for you tomorrow with the best lawyer he has ever dealt with."

"I do thank you, and please convey my appreciation to your wife. I wish I hadn't asked the journey of her."

"You didn't ask it of her. In fact, you seemed to do your best to discourage her from coming. But you can convey your well wishes yourself when you call on her before or after your appointment. I beg of you not to leave me to tell her, as I am certain to not have an answer to all the questions she'll have for me. And wild horses couldn't have kept her from Town, so don't let that trouble you in the least."

“Might she be up to accompanying us to speak with the lawyers then, do you suppose?”

“If you were to invite her, nothing could keep her away, I can assure you.”

Eve laughed, feeling a trifle restored after the ugly confrontation with Sabina. “Would you mind? Under the circumstances, I know you would prefer she not exert herself.”

“I wouldn’t allow her to walk, that’s certain. But I will be by her side, and yours, so, no, if you are comfortable with having a crowd with you, we will both be delighted to accompany you.”

“Hardly a crowd,” Eve countered with another slight laugh. “Just the three of us and Mr. Smythe.” She paused for a moment and another thought occurred to her. “Does your father think to accompany us? Still not a crowd, but it might start to feel cramped in the solicitor’s office.”

“While I’m sure he is now curious about why I asked him for a referral, no, I don’t think we will include him this time. If we need him, we’ll save that for future reference.”

This time Eve’s laughter felt more genuine. It was still new for her to feel she had the backing of people who didn’t have ulterior motives for helping her. But she was quickly coming to enjoy the experience.

If only she hadn’t been so foolish as to have run away from them. But they didn’t seem to be holding it against her, she realized with relief.

Evangeline returned home late and then managed to escape the house the next morning all without encountering Sabina or Ralph. It surprised her after the scene Sabina played out before her at the rout.

Eve still didn’t know how Sabina had managed to get in after Eve had refused to arrange an invitation for her. Why had Sabina bothered to ask her if she already had made arrangements? And why were they so determined to marry her off?

Surely they weren't truly so daft as to think Eve marrying a nobleman could help them in some way, even if they claimed that to be their reason. Or at least, why now? Why were they trying so hard, now, to match her? Was it just because Eve had finally left of mourning?

It took effort to shake off the disquieting thoughts, but Eve did what had to be done in order to have her mind clear for the meeting with the solicitor that day. She had arrived at Everleigh House much earlier than was fashionable but had been received politely by the butler who had been expecting her.

Very quickly Lucy arrived and welcomed her with enthusiasm.

"I do apologize that I didn't remain in attendance last night. I was impressed to learn that you stayed quite late. You are far more resilient than I."

"I am not in an interesting condition," Eve excused, embarrassed by the praise.

"The drive to Town isn't so arduous when in a comfortable carriage. But I didn't feel like facing the crowds last night. I felt as though I was letting you down, though."

"I beg you, pay it no mind. Roderick and Sean were there and ensured I was well cared for, especially when Sabina turned up and was up to her usual tricks of matchmaking. We managed not to cause any scenes, but I'm afraid she might have been vulgar with poor Mr. Smythe."

"Sean would have likely found that reassuring to his thoughts on the English, so it was a favor to him more than anything, I'm sure."

Eve laughed. "The poor fellow does have just cause for his feelings from what I have heard."

Lucy shook her head. "Such a generalization is rather unacceptable within the scientific community. I am surprised he would allow himself to stick with such a prejudice for this long, especially now that he has made friends in England. He ought to have enough evidence that he has misjudged an entire nation by now."

"The wounds of childhood run deep."

Suddenly Lucy's smile broadened.

"You are quick to defend him."

Lucy's expression was sly but Eve ignored it. Now was not the time to become sidetracked. She needed to remain focused on why she was there.

"Gladys should be arriving soon with the box of paperwork. We thought it best if she brought it. No one would question her carrying one of my hatboxes. It would be perfectly natural that she take some things for service or some such. If I were to leave the house carrying anything, there would be much higher risk of one of the servants or household members questioning me. And I don't wish to deal with them until we've had our consultation."

"Of course," Lucy answered immediately. "But I'll be much more settled on your behalf once she has arrived."

Eve laughed again. "You seem to be taking this even more seriously than I am."

Her amusement died and a frown spread across her brow. "Are you still laboring under some burden of guilt that you wed your husband when he had a nearly non-existent passing thought that I might make a good match for him? I can assure you, I do not harbour any sort of feelings toward him nor did I ever. You have been married longer than I have been comfortable in Society. I'm not even thinking thoughts of remarriage now, let alone six or ten months ago. I beg of you to put such thoughts from your head."

Lucy's smile was gentle when she turned it upon Eve. "I just want to do you a good turn, Evangeline. It's what friends do."

"I have no experience with that, but I will accept your word. It is much more palatable than thinking you are trying to pay me back for thinking you've stolen something from me. You certainly have not. While I'm sure your husband is perfectly lovely, I don't think he would be the man for me even if I were thinking of marriage for myself."

"Perhaps more a confused Scot?" Lucy asked with a droll wiggle of her eyebrows. Eve didn't bother rejecting the other woman's words as she was too busy laughing.

It was exactly perfect for her as she needed the light-hearted moment before her meeting with the solicitor. Nerves fluttered in her midsection as Roderick and Sean entered the receiving room to collect her and Lucy.

"It's time, my lady," Sean said solemnly as he bowed over her hand. "Your maid has arrived and all is in readiness."

The flutters changed their nature slightly and she grew warm rather than the chill that had pervaded her before. Her smile felt tremulous as she stood and tucked her hand into his elbow for the walk to the carriage.

Before she could fully collect her wits, she was being settled into a big chair in front of the suitably solemn-looking and non-descript Mr. Brown. Roderick Northcott had been assured by his father, the Earl of Everleigh, that Mr. Brown was the most knowledgeable and dependable solicitor for matters pertaining to property ownership. Evangeline hoped they hadn't been too vague with the earl for his recommendation to carry the appropriate weight.

"I was sorry to learn of your loss Mrs. Robertson," Mr. Brown began. "Or do you prefer to be called Lady

Evangeline? I tend toward legalities, of course, but I know you have the courtesy of a title."

Eve waved a hand to dismiss the question. "Whatever you are comfortable with, sir. I have never been addressed as Mrs. Robertson, but under the circumstances, it is appropriate."

The man nodded before examining some papers on his desk in front of him. He looked at her over the rim of his glasses. Eve had the impression that he was a scholarly type, like he would be more at home in a classroom than a courtroom. But then his gaze turned very shrewd and she wondered if he could read her thoughts.

"Very well," he began, possibly in acknowledgement of her words about how to address her, she couldn't be perfectly certain. Nerves reared up once more. "When we received his lordship's message requesting that we represent you, we took the liberty of doing a little digging into your circumstances in order to understand your background and why you might be requiring a solicitor."

Eve frowned. "Wasn't that a waste of time without knowing the details from me?"

"No," he answered firmly, without apology. "It is better to come to a few of our own conclusions first, especially in high profile matters."

"Oh, I don't think this is something that will be terribly important or –"

He cut her off. "I don't mean to be rude to you, Mrs. Robertson, but I can assure you, this will be very high profile. You are here about your husband's properties and businesses, aren't you?"

Eve glanced at Roderick to see if perhaps he had told the lawyers more than she had thought, but he appeared as taken aback as she felt. She was comforted by a touch on her shoulder that she knew was from

Sean. She didn't look at him, though. She needed all her wits trained upon the solicitor.

"Well, yes, that is what I wish to discuss with you, but while it might be a challenge to extricate matters from Ralph and Sabina, it surely isn't going to be a very involved process."

"I can assure you it is," Mr. Brown countered. "Are you not aware of the extent of your husband's holdings?"

"I know of some of them. There are several properties with mining interests and there was his lending house, of course, too. And I suppose the shipping." She trailed off, realizing suddenly that the solicitor might very well be right.

"The lending house is one of the biggest issues as there are many interesting names included on the list of clients. But it is likely you don't know even a fraction of your husband's interests and possessions. We haven't reached the limits of what he was involved in and we have been searching already for a couple of days."

He nodded approvingly over Eve's stunned expression, as though he were pleased with her silence. "Now, show me what you've brought. I assume you wish to ensure your husband's family ceases their interference."

Again, Eve was shocked into silence. She knew for certain Roderick wouldn't have passed on that part of the matter as it was of the utmost importance that it remain confidential.

Again, it was as though the man read her thoughts.

"Have no fear, Mrs. Robertson. Our firm conducts itself with the utmost discretion. Our investigation has been entirely private, and we haven't discussed your personal business with anyone, especially not your late husband's family."

Silence filled the room as Evangeline and her companions all looked at one another in disbelief. Suddenly the lawyers dour face broke into a grin.

"This is the part of my job I enjoy the most. Surprising fine, upstanding folks with how shady some things can be. But I promise you, I am completely above board. I just wanted to know what I was dealing with before meeting with you. Any friend of Everleigh is a friend of our firm, and I wanted to give you the best service I could. I find that knowing a bit of background first makes that easier."

Eve still felt a bit shaky, but what did she know? She had never had business to conduct or a lawyer to confer with. It would seem the others were just as surprised as she was, but they too were likely nearly as inexperienced as she. And it did make a certain kind of sense what he was saying. She finally nodded.

"Since it seems like you already know everything, is our presence here superfluous or do you need anything from me?"

"Your presence is far from superfluous, my lady. I need to know what sort of evidentiary papers you might have in your possession and which of your husband's holdings you have access to."

Eve gestured and Gladys hurried forward with the box she had been clutching to her chest the entire time she stood at the back of the room with her wide eyes staring in wonder. Evangeline wondered if she had a similar expression plastered on her own features.

She smiled reassuringly at her maid, thanking her quietly for the paperwork. Sean quickly stepped forward to take it from her hands and brought it to the lawyer's desk.

"You have been diligent," he complimented.

"I had a great deal of help," Eve replied modestly and truthfully. She wouldn't be there without the assistance of the other occupants of the room.

"Tell me what you currently understand of the situation," Mr. Brown prompted as he opened the box and started pulling out the reams of paper.

"We found what seems to be the settlement papers when Gerald and my father negotiated our marriage. Also, what might be his will. Both seem to indicate that he was entrusting me to inherit his possessions in the event of his death."

"All of them?" Mr. Brown asked.

"That is my understanding," she replied. "Or rather, there wasn't a listing differentiating between various heirs. We did come across deeds to a few properties, such as a house I had admired not long before Gerald's death."

Mr. Brown was nodding as she spoke, but his attention was clearly focused on the papers in his hands.

"It isn't that unusual, Mrs. Robertson. In spheres other than the one you're used to, it is often the case that immediate family inherits everything a man has worked for. It is only the aristocracy with their titles and entailed properties that things can go in different and perhaps odd directions."

Mr. Brown paused and stared at her over his glasses once more.

"You never suspected you were the heiress because you are a noblewoman, and it isn't usual in your Society. But it is very likely your husband's family was aware of your ignorance and used it to their advantage. And of course, with your being a woman."

Eve nodded and blinked away the burn of tears at the back of her throat. It shouldn't be a shock to her. It was what they had surmised. But she had hoped the lawyer would somehow disprove their suspicions. How could the Robertsons have thought to displace her like that?

And what was she going to do with all Gerald's wealth?

"What can we do about it? How do I enforce my ownership if Ralph has taken over everything?"

"I suppose you don't want to have him arrested? That would be the easiest route to take. And you are well within your rights both legally and even morally to do so."

"No, I cannot think Gerald would have wanted me to so mistreat them. He thought they were fools which is, I suppose, why he dispensed with his holdings in this way, but I can't think he would want them to be jailed for their trickery."

"It's more than trickery, ma'am. They have stolen incredible wealth from you."

"It could be argued that they haven't. Which is likely what their solicitor would argue, isn't it? They didn't actually take anything from me. Ralph could argue that he has merely been assisting me. I was so shocked by Gerald's death, and I never thought to be his heir, so I didn't even think about running the businesses. I don't even know what all he owned, as you already pointed out."

The solicitor smiled at her as though she were a pleasant simpleton. Perhaps she was.

Eve almost burst into hysterical laughter but managed to keep her reactions under control. They finalized the meeting and Eve got to her feet. The solicitor's tread was heavy as he came around his desk as she took her leave.

"Don't work yourself into a taking over this, Mrs. Robertson. We will have it all arranged quite promptly. I would suggest you find somewhere else to stay for a few days while we have the other residents of your home evicted."

"Oh, no, that is not what I wish at all. Oh bother. We didn't really discuss my intentions." Eve sat back down with a plop. "I am allowing things to be managed for me, once again."

Squaring her shoulders, Eve looked the solicitor in the eye and watched as he returned to his side of the desk and resumed his seat.

"I would like to arrange a settlement with Ralph. Not an exceedingly generous settlement, but I have no desire to leave them destitute either. I don't think Town agrees with them, but if they are determined to remain in the city, they can have Gerald's house. I never liked it and have no desire to retain it. They already have property of their own in their home village, so that should suffice for them. And some sort of financial settlement. Or perhaps if it can be ascertained which business he might be successful at running, we could make that over to him."

As she spoke, Mr. Brown's eyebrows rose incrementally, as though his estimation of her was increasing with them. He nodded slightly and took notes as she spoke.

"Also, if it is established that I do in fact own Gerald's interests, I will need assistance in running them. If that is within the realm of your expertise, I would be interested in retaining your services. If it is not, if you could recommend a firm to me, that would be most helpful. Mr. Smythe has agreed to be retained as my advisor in economic matters, please arrange for his information so that he can be suitably compensated for his efforts."

"Very well, my lady," the gentleman said, nodding firmly. "We can arrange all of that."

"How soon can it be done?"

"How soon can you find somewhere else to stay?" he countered with his eyebrow still elevated.

"By this evening, I dare say. It might be irregular, but we could stay at one of the better hotels, myself and my maid."

"Absolutely not," Lucy finally spoke for the first time in the entire interview. "You will stay at Everleigh House with us. It will be remarked upon less than staying at any hotel, even a decent one."

"Thank you, Lucy, that is generous. Hopefully we can arrange for my removal to the other house as quickly as possible."

"The one on Spring Street that you'd mentioned?"

"Yes," Eve nodded.

"I will make that a priority then."

Eve regained her feet, this time more decisively than the first. "Thank you, Mr. Brown. Shall we say I will return in three days to see how things are progressing?"

"That will do," he agreed in his usual monotone, but Eve could see the light of amusement in his brown gaze, as though he had realized there was more to the young widow than he had originally thought.

Mr. Brown fixed his glare upon Roderick just as Eve was about to turn from the room.

"You be certain to keep watch over this one, Mr. Northcott. She will be a target and is too special to be allowed an injury."

Her laughter followed her out of the room. A target? She hadn't thought the serious lawyer to be so fanciful.

Chapter Nineteen

Sean hadn't known where to look at the end of the interview with the lawyer. All he wanted to do was sweep Evangeline from the room and off to Scotland where he would be in a better position to protect her from the maelstrom that was going to crash over her soon.

"It's better that you'll be at Everleigh, Evangeline," he said to her as soon as they gained the street. "I wasn't comfortable with you returning to that house after the rout last night, but now that the lawyer is fully involved, you should never be alone with any of the other Robertsons."

"I really can't imagine that any of them would offer me a physical injury," Eve protested.

"You didn't think they would steal from you, either, did you?"

"No." Her answer came in a small voice as though she didn't want to admit it even to herself. The urge to comfort her increased in bounds.

"I can walk you home if you'd rather not take a hack," he offered, knowing of her penchant for walking.

"Would you really?" Her voice was so eager, and her open face did nonsensical things to his innards.

After a nod exchanged with Roderick and without another word, Sean took Evangeline's hand into the crook of his elbow and set off toward her street.

It would take them a good while to get there but he had nowhere else he needed to be that day. The Northcott townhouse wasn't terribly conducive to studying, and he didn't expect he would be able to concentrate with Eve's issues up in the air.

They weren't his problem, he tried to tell himself. He could return to the estate and continue his studies. Except this was the most interesting thing he had taken on since he shifted his focus to mathematics and economies.

It really was a perfect scenario for his focused attention. Except he knew that he was even more fascinated with the woman than the numbers she was associated with.

Gallantly, though, he tried to keep his riotous thoughts to himself. It wasn't the lady's fault he found her so fascinating. He couldn't inflict all the questions in his head upon her. She wasn't a subject for study.

But how he wished she were.

"Thank you, Mr. Smythe. Even though the air isn't nearly so fresh here in Town, I just needed to be out and catch my breath."

"I know. You would often take walks when we were together on the estate. It seemed every time there were powerful things, whether good or bad, you would head out for a stroll. Do you find it is the walking or the distance that helps you?"

Eve's laugh was a relief to Sean. It sounded like one of her real ones, not a forced or fake fluff of air to hide what she was really feeling. It seemed she was relaxing as she always did when she walked.

"I have never considered the matter. I believe it is the movement, so the act of walking. It is a distraction from whatever is feeling overwhelming in the moment. As you said, either good things or bad things. There is peace in walking. Even in the city."

She paused in thought before adding, "It is possible, though, that it is as you suggested, a way to gain distance from the thing, too. Or as in this case, a delaying tactic."

She laughed again, and it took all Sean's considerable will power to remain steadily by her side rather than pulling her tighter into the crook of his arm.

"What are you delaying?" he asked without thought, and then had to laugh at his own expense when she cast him such a look of incredulity. "Ah, of course, you don't wish to have a confrontation with the other Mrs. Robertson."

"Exactly. I managed to come home after her last night and leave the house this morning without encountering her. But between the ugliness last night and the knowledge I now carry about her future, I fear any engagement with her at this point."

"Perhaps you shouldn't return at all. Your maid," Sean gestured behind them where the woman was trailing them, "could surely collect whatever you might require and bring it for you to Everleigh House."

"Doesn't that strike you as decidedly craven?"

"Not at all, it seems prudent to me."

She lowered her voice and nearly whispered the words, "What if something were to happen to Gladys?"

A shiver ran through Sean, but not one of fear. Spotting a small grassy area with a bench slightly secluded by a shrubby tree, he pulled her over and took a seat.

"Do you actually fear for either of your safety?" he demanded, incredulous. "I thought it was merely an uncomfortable situation you would have to deal with if you came face-to-face with any of your late husband's family. What do you think might happen?"

"We are discussing a great deal of money here, Sean. Surely you realize people regularly do horrible things for just a fraction of the amounts likely involved in my husband's holdings."

Sean wanted to repeat the word late that ought to have gone before the word husband in her case. She was no longer wed to the man. And from what he could tell, Gerald had been a terrible match for her. He was greedy and domineering, harsh and controlling. None of those descriptions could be applied to Lady Evangeline.

Even when he had first made her acquaintance when she was cold and reserved. She had still been one who showed consideration for others. And despite her previous cool collection, he didn't think she would have been well equipped to handle the bullying she likely had received from all the Robertsons since her marriage.

It was a good thing she was a widow. What would he have done if he had met her and she wasn't one? Not that he knew what to do with her now, but he thought he might have been tempted to violence if he had met her in company of her *late* husband.

He dragged his thoughts back to the discussion at hand when he realized she was watching him expectantly.

"Of course people do horrible things. Just consider the horrible thing the family has done by not telling you about your options for independence. The fact that they had the audacity to move into your home and take over your businesses reveals their true motives. But have you known them to ever be violent?"

"No, but my judgment isn't reliable in this case, as I clearly never really knew them in the first place."

Her voice had grown softer and he had to lean closer to hear what she was saying. Her face was bowed over her lap as though she were weighed down by it all.

Suddenly, though, she lifted her head to look at him and to Sean's shocked delight their faces were only millimetres apart. His breath caught in his throat and he froze with indecision.

It would take barely half a thought to lean forward and settle his lips on hers where they sat, slightly parted, just below his face. But he couldn't shame her in such a way, not in public. Despite his desire to stare at her mouth for the rest of the day, he lifted his gaze to enmesh with her own.

He could see from their wide, dazed expression that she was nearly as surprised by the development as he was. But she wasn't repulsed by the possibility either. At least he didn't think so

Suddenly, her tongue reached out as though of its own volition to moisten her lips, and Sean nearly groaned with his desire. That brought him to his senses almost like the splash of cold water on a hot flame. He straightened away from her, clearing his throat and tugging on his cravat.

What had they been discussing before his brain melted? Ah yes, was it craven to avoid the Robertsons until matters were cleared up.

"If there is the least possibility of trouble, you ought to remain far from your home. If you think your maid won't even be safe, then send some footmen with instructions for another maid to gather what you need. Or Roderick and I can escort your maid. But you are not to go there."

Suddenly Eve's gaze, which had been warm and soft with budding interest, grew firm and cooled considerably.

"You cannot give me orders, Mr. Smythe."

"No, of course not, I'm sorry for my impertinence, but please let us remain on good terms. Don't starch up and call me mister. I am merely watching out for your safety."

She thawed slightly but still held herself carefully away from him as though regretting the almost incident that had just passed.

"I appreciate that – Sean. Thank you."

She stumbled over his name but still managed to keep the informality. For that, Sean would be grateful.

"And I'm certain you have the right of it. It would be foolish of me to put myself in harm's way just to prove that no one is the lord of me any longer."

"So shall we head to Everleigh House, then?" Sean stood and offered her his elbow once more. After a barely noticeable hesitation she took his arm and stepped up close to him.

Chapter Twenty

Had they nearly kissed?

Evangeline couldn't get her mind to function properly for the rest of their walk. It was beyond scandalous but decadently delicious. Her innards squirmed with the flutters of a hundred butterflies and her limbs felt loose and warm. And yet nothing untoward had even happened.

What a silly reaction.

He was merely expressing concern over her. As a gentleman ought to do.

He was a sweet, kind man. An intelligent one at that. If she were the least bit interested in falling in love, she could see that he might be a perfect candidate. But she wasn't, of course.

What folly that would be. Especially at such a pivotal point in her life.

No, she needed to remain focused on business. The businesses she was about to take over, of course. She needed to find out the extent of them, for one thing.

The solicitor would do much of that, she was certain, but she could find out some too if she could gain access to some of Gerald's offices. She at least knew that Gerald had conducted much of his dealings at the lending house. She would start there as soon as it had been secured from Ralph.

In the meantime, Sean was right, she would stay away from all Robertsons until matters were sorted by the solicitors. It wasn't cowardly, it was wise.

But she couldn't put Gladys at risk either. Or should she send the woman with footmen? Eve resolved to ask the woman as soon as they were off the street.

"Of course, I'll go arrange your things, m'lady," Gladys exclaimed as soon as they had reached the room they had been assigned and she was assisting Eve in tidying herself. "I already assembled much of what would be required before we left, as I assumed we would be removing ourselves at least temporarily."

"You are far wiser than I, Gladys," Eve complimented as she watched the servant's nimble fingers straighten her curls with remarkable skill. "I was most fortunate when Gerald arranged for you to care for me."

Gladys grinned into the mirror but didn't make another response.

Eve sighed and shifted her position slightly, trying to get comfortable.

"Are you overwrought, m'lady? It has been a trying day, I'm sure."

"I wouldn't say overwrought," Eve began with a slight laugh. "But it has been vexing, to be frank."

"Why vexing?"

"I didn't think of delays. I thought we would see a solicitor and all would be sorted. It was not well thought out of me, I'm afraid. But now I realize that the solicitor's foresight will actually speed up the process and yet, it will still linger."

"It was good of him to have begun his investigations even before your visit to explain matters."

"A trifle presumptuous of him, though, wouldn't you say?"

Gladys' reflection grinned again. "I think that is lawyers' forte, wouldn't you say? They have to presume all manner of things to get to the bottom of matters."

"Perhaps," Eve answered grudgingly, still feeling a little grumpy about the entire matter. She supposed her dissatisfaction could be attributed to her uncertain feelings in other arenas as well, but that was not to be thought of.

"I recognize it's not my place to monitor your associations, m'lady, but do have a care."

Eve met Gladys' gaze with a frown. "Which associations are you talking about? You just agreed it is better that we stay here."

"It isn't the Northcotts I'm concerned about, but that Scotsman of theirs."

"We are a united kingdom now, Gladys," Eve said with amusement evident in her tone.

"That is merely politics. It doesn't change people's natures."

"No, I suppose it doesn't. Do you know he has very similar concerns about the lot of us? He finds it terribly challenging to trust anyone English."

Gladys bristled over that but never ceased in her ministrations. Finally, with a nod and one last pin, Gladys stepped back from the mirror.

"You are a wise lady, and I trust your judgment for the most part. But you aren't very old and have, from what I can tell, never had anyone to advise you properly since your mother died when you were a little girl. You must have a care. You are a very wealthy woman now, or will be soon enough. All manner of fools will be chasing you for your purse, and you could end up in a worse state than before."

"I might not be old, but I have experience now, Gladys. I appreciate your concerns, truly I do, and I thank you for caring to utter them. While I will admit, secretly, to you that Mr. Smythe does cause flutters in the region where I suspect my heart resides, now is far from an appropriate time for me to be so distracted."

"The heart wants what the heart wants, m'lady. Even your considerable will might not be sufficient to stop it in its tracks."

Eve laughed. "After the experiences I've had in life thus far, I wonder if the heart might be a wiser organ. My father didn't use his heart when he wed me with Gerald. And he certainly didn't when he squandered the entire family fortune, making said marriage necessary. Not that his misuse of his family's coffers was prompted by sense, either. Far from it."

Eve sighed. "I think now is not the time for matters of the heart, but I'm trying very hard not to ignore mine anymore. I went for too long closed off from people. You helped me see the error of that way."

Gladys appeared torn in her reaction to her mistress' words. Eve's lips twitched as she considered the maid. Obviously, she was pleased to have been of assistance, but she disapproved of what Eve might do now that she was opening herself up to other relationships.

"See that you don't go too far in the other direction, though, m'lady. It wouldn't do to court scandal now that you're just about to come into your windfall."

Eve giggled. Actually giggled. She didn't know she could make such a noise. Perhaps she *would* become scandalous along with the windfall.

But no, if Eve knew one thing about herself, it was that she was the conventional sort. She would not be courting scandal any time soon, not if she could prevent it, in any case. Her sigh accompanied the thought.

She really was a boring old soul.

But that night, her decision to avoid scandal was put to the test. And it wasn't even her fault.

"We don't need a Scotsman born on the wrong side of the blanket sullying up our drawing rooms, sir."

Eve blinked over the harsh words, not realizing what exactly they meant but sensing Sean's distress from the stiffening of his arm where her hand lay on it as he was escorting her to the dancefloor.

"Was he talking to you?" she asked in a voice barely over a whisper.

"He was," Sean answered in a tone that couldn't hide his anger.

"But you weren't," she stumbled over the scandalous words. She couldn't actually repeat what had been uttered.

"My father annulling his marriage with my mother means that I was."

Eve's indrawn breath sounded like a hiss. Sean must have mistaken her meaning. He stiffened further. "Would you have me escort you back to Lucy or would you prefer I just walk away immediately?"

Eve frowned. "Neither," she exclaimed, confused. "Why would you think to leave me on my own? Because of what that buffoon said? It is likely he had a trifle too much of the punch. I shan't pay him the least mind."

"Your loyalty might lead you into trouble."

"I don't care for the friendship of fools," Eve countered. "If someone can't be bothered to find out the facts before they form an opinion, or merely pass on juicy slander they've heard, that disqualifies them from my good opinion."

Approval shined in Sean's gaze as he swept her through the movements of the waltz. The newly popular dance was still a challenge for Evangeline, who wasn't very experienced in socializing, so she had to concentrate, lest she miss the steps.

But it was a thrill to feel herself swept around the room in a whirl of music and swirling colours caused by the glowing candlelight flickering over the gowns of the other ladies.

"You are the most beautiful woman present, my lady." She noticed his burr was far more pronounced when he was being earnest. Evangeline's heart fluttered even as her nerves tightened. Now wasn't the time.

She barely knew the time was passing until the music came to an end and she returned to reality with a bit of a thud in the form of Sabina on the arm of another viscount she was trying to pawn off on Eve.

"What are you doing with this gentleman once more?" Sabina hissed at her.

"I could ask you the same question," Eve countered with an impish feeling welling within herself.

She wasn't beholden to the Robertsons any longer. Her lawyer was going to prove that soon enough. She had never been under obligation to entertain Sabina's strange compulsion to arrange a marriage for her. But now even less so.

"If you've finished with this one, you ought to partner with Viscount Connell."

"Surely the gentleman can speak for himself," Eve returned firmly but offered an apologetic smile to the gentleman in question.

"I would be honored, my lady." The viscount bowed elegantly.

Eve stifled her sigh. She couldn't avoid the invitation without causing a stir. She dipped a curtsy to Sean and then took the other gentleman's arm as the next cotillion was struck.

"I would have preferred a waltz," he said with a smile. "But this will do."

"Why are you doing Mrs. Robertson's bidding, my lord?" Eve boldly asked the question, throwing caution to the wind. The gentleman looked at her as though she had lost her mind, and Eve couldn't argue with him. Perhaps she had.

"I do no one's bidding except my own, my dear lady. If I didn't think you were overwrought, I would take exception to your words."

Eve blinked and nearly laughed. Overwrought? No doubt Sabina had dropped that hint, or perhaps the gossips. What was she to say to such an explanation?

"I meant you no insult, my lord. Do accept my apology. I was merely surprised to be introduced to you by Mrs. Robertson."

The viscount lifted his eyebrows at her before they lowered into a frown. "She said she was responsible for you."

Now it was Eve's turn to frown, even as she followed him in the steps of the dance. "Responsible for me? How perfectly odd. I wonder what she meant by that."

Lord Connell didn't appear to be terribly concerned about the matter. "I assumed she meant because of your being a young woman, like she was your chaperone or something. She is your family, isn't she? Is that not usual in families?"

Eve tried not to snort in response. For one thing, even though she had been referring to the Robertsons as "the family" she hadn't ever thought of them as her own family. They didn't treat her how she expected family ought to treat each other. Not that what little family she had treated her as she thought family ought. But Sabina being her chaperone carried an odd thought for her. And a flutter of guilt started up in her insides.

Was she a beast for considering turning the Robertsons out on their ears? Perhaps they really did want the best for her.

Of course, they had also stolen her inheritance. Eve didn't know what to think. But the beauty of it was, she didn't have to decide then and there. She resolved to enjoy the rest of the evening. She could ponder the rest on the morrow.

Chapter Twenty-One

Sean had to work hard at not glaring across the room as Evangeline went through the steps of the dance with Viscount Connell. The scientist in him was rather horrified over the barbaric tendency that was urging him to stomp across the room and pull his woman from the other man's arms.

For one thing, Sean tried to reason with himself, she wasn't his woman. At most she was his friend. He had no call to feel so possessive of her. But for another, she would not welcome the scandalous display of ownership. And finally, if looked at objectively, no one could argue that there was anything questionable about her dancing with the viscount.

It wasn't an overly suggestive dance. The steps didn't even bring them into salaciously close contact.

And still Sean wanted to pull Eve into his arms and run from the room with her.

He had obviously turned into a simpleton.

Just standing on the edge of the room staring after her was going to cause gossip if he didn't get himself under control. Sure enough, Lucy was making her way toward him.

Sean could tell she was trying very hard not to appear as though she were stalking toward him. He doubted anyone but her closest friends would notice the glimmer of anger hiding behind her Society appropriate smile.

"What are you glaring about, Sean?" Lucy didn't bother asking him any leading questions. She got straight to the point.

"I had no knowledge of doing so, Mrs. Northcott," Sean replied in as bland a tone as he could muster, not really interested in entertaining a lecture from her at the moment.

Under other circumstances he found her attempts at instruction to be quaint and amusing. This wasn't likely to be one of those times.

"You are going to draw gossip down upon all of our heads," Lucy continued, ignoring his statement. "If you cannot behave appropriately, perhaps you ought to return home."

Sean felt as though she had slapped him. While he recognized that he might be somewhat irrational in his attraction toward Lady Evangeline, he never would have thought Lucy would be so enamoured with her new project that she would turn her ire upon him.

He stiffened to his full height and nodded politely to his best friend's wife. "That shan't be necessary, ma'am."

"Don't get all starchy with me," Lucy exclaimed in a low tone, leaning in close to speak to him quietly, so as not to be overheard. "You know you are a member of our family, and nothing will ever change that. But right now, we have to focus on what's best for Evangeline, not ourselves."

"I had no intention of doing anything to harm the woman."

"Inviting gossip about her by intimidating any other suitors isn't going to deter any talk about her, Sean. I know you aren't so oblivious to polite company as to not know that."

Sean couldn't help but be amused at Lucy's dry tone. She wasn't wrong. That was likely why he hated her censure so much. He agreed with her.

"Did you know Mrs. Ralph Robertson might be here?"

"No, how could any of us expect that?" Lucy asked with a huff of dismay. "Poor Evie. Her nerves must be stretched thin. There is no way that any of us could have expected to encounter any of them here."

Suddenly Lucy's eyes widened. "Have you seen the sons? Are they here as well?"

"You have the light of another project gleaming in your eyes, Lucy. I don't think Roderick will tolerate your taking on those two."

Lucy laughed. "It was a fleeting idea. But I couldn't possibly."

"Would it be too big a challenge for you?"

Lucy's outraged gasp amused Sean, but she quickly disabused him of his outrageous idea.

"It is certainly not that," she exclaimed with a huff. "It is the fact that they were most likely complicit in the theft from Evangeline. As her friend, I couldn't possibly be so disloyal as to turn around and assist the villains, despite the temptation of the possibilities."

Sean tried hard not to bark with laughter. That would surely draw far too much attention to him. Attention he did not want. For one thing, he was well aware that it would draw uninvited ire upon him as had already happened that evening.

That reminder did the opposite of what it normally would do, though. It warmed Sean's heart when he remembered how Evie reacted to the charlatan's rough words. Even if she hadn't understood them, which he was nearly certain she had, the tone would have told her they weren't attractive nor complimentary. But she had carried on with him to the dance floor and seemingly enjoyed her time in his arms.

The waltz. The words would never mean the same thing to him after dancing it with her.

Now he was turning into a poet. That was for a different scholarly society, he assured himself, fighting another grin.

"You do not seem to be your usual moody self, Sean. Are you well?"

Now Sean did laugh, but he kept the volume low. "I'm not grumpy, so I must be unwell?"

Colour stained Lucy's cheeks and she returned his grin, but she didn't withdraw her words.

"I didn't know your face could contain a smile that wasn't stained with sarcasm," she explained.

"Very descriptive, Lucy," Sean complimented before he finally answered her question. "I am very well, I thank you for your concern."

"You aren't falling in love with her, are you?" Lucy asked suddenly, seeming worried about the topic.

"Aren't you the one who was trying to play matchmaker?" Sean frowned.

"I was, but that was before I realized how very complicated it was going to be."

"You shouldn't start what you can't finish."

"Oh, I have no intention of stopping, I just don't think my first match was appropriate."

Sean felt as though Lucy had stabbed him deep into his heart. His shock must have displayed itself on his face. Why wouldn't it? It wasn't every day your closest friends abandon you. Although, for Sean, it was a distressingly frequent occurrence.

"Don't look like that Sean, I meant you no insult. I just didn't appreciate the extent of Society's discomfort with your situation. With the challenges Lady Evangeline faces, I think she might need less controversial partners by her side."

"You think to match her with someone else? Like who? Ellis?"

"Viscount Severn might be a good choice, but with Beaverbrook constantly searching for a new broodmare, Ellis draws nearly as much gossip as you."

Sean was going to argue with Lucy but she cut in before he could.

"Oh, bother, I never realized, our little group of students are all rather controversial, aren't we? I never really contemplated that before."

"You didn't?" Sean asked, taken aback. "What did you think setting up house with the likes of us was going to be? Even without any extra scandals, Roderick's efforts to make us money are going to cause gossip whether we invent something wonderful or not."

Lucy's sigh would have bowled him over if he weren't immune to dramatics. Instead, he grinned at her, unable to stay injured in the face of her misery.

"Have you fallen in love with her?" Now Lucy sounded almost hopeful about it, unlike her sentiments mere moments before.

"Were you faking to get my reaction?" Sean was aghast.

Lucy shrugged. "Mayhap."

Sean couldn't take the matter lightly, but he didn't hurl any inappropriate language at his best friend's wife. He couldn't think of her as his own friend in that moment, despite the fact that he had already forgiven her for her earlier words. The fact that they might have been said to stir up his other feelings was cruelty in his opinion. But he never would have thought Lucy capable of cruelty, so he just shook his head and turned away.

He had to check on Evangeline. He couldn't stand here and bandy words with a questionable friend.

Sean had been doing his best not to watch her with a glower as she danced with that ridiculous viscount her sister-in-law had matched her with. Viscount Connell wasn't so terrible, Sean would have thought in a different context. But he was not for Evangeline.

Then his nemesis approached. Why was this evening turning into a fiasco? First the rough words from someone he hadn't even identified. Or wait, had it been his cousin who had called them?

That shouldn't surprise him. His cousin was the sort who would say such things, to be sure. But it hadn't sounded like him.

Sean was familiar with Harlow's boorish tones despite the fact that he'd rather not even acknowledge the connection. That feeling was certainly mutual, Sean was sure.

"What do you want Harlow?" Sean asked as the man stopped beside him.

"I want to know why you've never visited."

"Visited who, pray tell?"

"Our grandparents, for one, your father, for another, and, well, me, to be quite frank."

"Why would I visit any of those people, you especially?"

"We are family."

"Not by my definition of the word."

"Then for a well-educated person you aren't very intelligent," Carrick replied with a smirk. "I would say any dictionary you chose to open would tell you that people related to one another by birth and blood are most definitely family."

"For the very important years between my fifth summer and my twentieth, none of you acknowledged my existence. The fact that your uncle has suddenly changed his mind and wishes to acknowledge he sired me doesn't alter what was done to me and what your Society now thinks of me. So again, I repeat, why would I ever visit any of you?"

Carrick smirked again but from what he could see from the corner of his eye because he refused to look at the man, Sean suspected there might be a thread of sincerity in him. As though his words had actually injured the other man. That was hardly possible, though, so he dismissed the wayward thought.

"I was a foolish boy when we were at school, Sean. You can't hold it against me forever."

"I can if I so wish. If not for Roderick Northcott and his friends, you would have made my existence worse than miserable when I was already having enough of my own struggles."

"You aren't the only boy to have struggles."

"Perhaps not, but I would argue that mine were deeper and more complicated than yours due to your uncle's actions. Yours only made them worse."

"Would you accept an apology at this point?"

Sean couldn't even fathom that Carrick Harlow would consider extending one, nor any of the rest of his family. While Sean's father had paid lip service to an apology, it was always to try to gain Sean's cooperation in some sort of scheme or situation.

Somehow, this felt different. But he didn't have time to dwell on the matter.

"I might consider it," Sean finally allowed. "But tonight is not the time and this event is not the place."

"Will you call on me then?" Carrick asked in a low voice as Sean turned to walk away.

Sean didn't bother acknowledging the other man's words, but he felt slightly warmed by them anyhow. But he hadn't been lying to the man. This was not the time for the complicated conversation that would be required for any sort of reconciliation between the cousins.

He needed to keep his focus on Evangeline and her more urgent and current matter. Sean's illegitimacy was a long-standing matter that could wait a bit longer.

The interlude with Harlow had caused him to lose sight of Eve and it took considerable effort to search the rooms without appearing to do so. Subterfuge and delicacy had never been his strong suit, but he managed not to stir up any more scandal than his own presence could contribute. He finally found her by the refreshment table, accepting a glass of punch from one of the attentive servants.

"You should have had one of your swains fetch that for you," Sean said in place of a greeting.

Evangeline's eyes lit up and her lips twisted into a form of sarcastic amusement. But instead of laughter, all that came from her was a sigh that she tried to hide behind the rim of her glass.

"Was the dancing not to your taste?" Sean asked with a frown.

"Dancing is always lovely," Eve argued before adding, "Well, nearly always."

She sighed again.

"What has happened?"

Eve shook her head and didn't meet his gaze. "It's all just more of the same. Don't allow my fidgets to trouble you, I beg of you. I am merely impatient. Which is odd considering I allowed the last eighteen months to pass without even bothering with anything. Now, suddenly, I've turned my attention to the matter and want it resolved on the instant. It isn't very scholarly of me, is it?"

The little laugh she tacked on to the end of her question sounded forced to Sean's ears, but he was relieved that she was showing a bit of spirit.

"Scholars are nearly all some of the most impatient people you've ever met," Sean argued with a smile. "That is what usually prompts innovation. Someone says out loud or to themselves *I don't like how this thing works* so they come up with some new, better way of doing it."

"I don't know if the chemists would agree with you," Eve countered with a smile to show she wasn't actually picking a fight. "If I understood what Ellis was explaining to me, he is discovering things that didn't already exist. Or rather, they did, of course, exist, but no one knew about them."

"True, true," Sean agreed, nodding, and finding his admiration for her growing out of all bounds, "But you will note that it was likely impatience with something that did exist that led to the new discovery."

Eve's tinkle of laughter sounded with his words and Sean almost had to clutch his chest to try to control his heart from leaping from his chest into her keeping. Again with the poetic thoughts, he thought, and just managed not to snort in derision over his own foolishness.

"Very well, you've convinced me. And I thank you for it. I am also reminded that I will wish to pay another visit to the Scholarly Society once my personal business is settled. I would love to learn more about the studies of each of the scholars. When I was there this time, I was too preoccupied with my own project to pay sufficient attention to everyone else's."

Sean managed to dredge a smile from the closet of his good manners and didn't growl with jealousy over her intention to spend time with the other fellows. His face must have revealed something of his thoughts to her as her face fell slightly. Thankfully her next words revealed that she hadn't read his mind.

"You must wish you hadn't agreed to take me on. It will likely be boring for you to deal with the finances for business when you've been working on more scientific mathematics up until now. I swear to you, I shan't keep you longer than necessary. I should be able to hire a team of bookkeepers and accountants who can keep track of everything once you've figured it out and established things for me."

Sean ought to be delighted by her words, but instead he felt a trifle insulted by them. "I have no wish to be elsewhere at the moment. And you certainly didn't force me to accept."

"No, I suspect Lucy did," Evie agreed with a little laugh. "And I'm sorry for that."

"Don't be," Sean insisted. "I'm quite looking forward to the challenge before us. I am happy to be involved."

"Even though it forces you into English Society?"

Sean lifted a shoulder, unsure how to reassure her. She wasn't wrong. He could do without the English Society part. But he was more interested in her presence and helping her with her adventure than he was determined to stay away from the nobles of her Society.

It was a new thought for him, one that would take some time to get used to.

His eyes flickered toward his cousin. If he was going to change his feelings, perhaps he would be able to make peace with Harlow after all.

Chapter Twenty-Two

Evangeline had to force herself not to stare at the man before her. She shouldn't find him so appealing.

He was a distraction she didn't need at a time when all her faculties were required on the matter at hand. It was going to be hard enough to wrest control away from the Robertsons and establish herself as a business-woman.

Businesswoman.

Was that even a word?

She marvelled at the very thought, especially at the possibility of such a word applying to her. And Sean was going to help her. For that she needed to trust him. But for her, trust was such a seductive act.

She had trusted so few people in her life. She had come to trust Gladys, which was working out quite nicely. The thought of trusting Sean, though, brought all sorts of mad, fluttery additions into the matter. It was remarkably ridiculous and yet she was enjoying the sensation enough not to wish it to cease.

But was she clever enough to be able to learn to be a woman of business while also entertaining new and unusual sensations? That was a question that would need to be answered in the coming days.

Eve was tired of living in fear. She had been doing so, it felt like for her entire life, but was really only since her mother had died, so about half her life.

Eve nearly rolled her eyes. Did it matter when? It had been for much too long; that was the point.

Now she was going to forge ahead, forge through, forge new pathways for herself. Whether that would include Society, she was finding herself not really minding either way.

What had Society ever done for her?

Well, it was thanks to the *ton* that she knew the Northcotts, and for that she could not be regretful. Eve reminded herself of that as Gladys helped her prepare for another meeting with the solicitors.

A flurry of activity had taken place since the last big event she had attended where Sabina had insisted she dance with Viscount Connell. Since then, despite Sabina and Ralph both turning up at Everleigh House demanding she return home, Eve hadn't laid eyes on any of the Robertsons.

Gladys and the footmen had managed to get most of her personal belongings out of the house without incident, and Eve was safely ensconced with the Northcotts and some of their scholars at the Earl of Everleigh's London townhouse.

Roderick had dealt with Ralph when he and Sabina had come calling. The servants hadn't even asked her if she would receive them, but Eve couldn't avoid hearing Ralph's bellowing.

"You won't get away with this, Evangeline," Ralph had hollered even as the footmen were showing him to the door.

Eve wasn't entirely certain what exactly he was referring to as she hadn't yet met again with the solicitors. She was embarrassed that everyone else had heard it too, but she had managed to keep her chin elevated afterward despite the squirming sensation in her midsection from the shame.

There was sufficient space for everyone in Everleigh house, Eve marvelled as she glanced around the lovely room she had been assigned. It wasn't terribly old fashioned, but it wasn't up to the very latest trends either, she acknowledged even as she admired the cleanliness of the far less cluttered home. And despite how very large and grand it was, the place still felt like a home. Somehow.

Eve was determined to dissect how that might have been managed. She wanted to be able to accomplish that for herself in whatever dwelling she ended up. She still hoped it would be the house on Spring Street, but at this point, she didn't much care as long as it wasn't Gerald's house.

A surge of guilt accompanied that thought, but she refused to give in to it. She was going to be happy. Eve was certain Gerald wouldn't begrudge her that. And she truly was grateful to Gerald for what he had done for her and her family.

She had learned enough now about economies from Sean that she understood what the infusion of cash Gerald provided to her father and brother would have done for her family's prospects. And from what she had also heard from others, it would seem her brother had managed to hold onto those better prospects and even improve upon them.

One of the scholars, Lincoln, was at this moment visiting her brother again to review his animal husbandry program and crop rotations. Eve had trouble imagining her brother having such a conversation, but she was ready to admit she didn't much know her sibling anymore. Perhaps she never had. It was a lowering thought but she pushed it from her mind.

The future was before her. She would do better with that. There wasn't anything to be done about the past.

But how to get through the coming confrontations? That was what troubled her currently.

With her stomach clenching, Eve had refused any breakfast other than a bit of toast and a few sips of tea. It wouldn't do to cast up her accounts in front of her rather intimidating solicitor. She knew he had tried to be kind to her. And he had been, in a rather severe way. But with all the changes and even her excitement about the future, it was all much too unsettled for her state of mind. Or perhaps for her state of stomach, she thought with wry amusement as she surveyed Gladys' handiwork in the mirror.

"As always, you've made me look better than I deserve," Eve remarked at Gladys' reflection.

"Go on with you, m'lady. Why would you say it like that?"

Eve sighed. "I feel quite dreadful and yet from how you've made me look, no one will be able to tell. I'm truly grateful for your skills, but it is still quite odd. I feel as though I don't deserve to look so well when I'm about to take everything away from Ralph and Sabina."

"We've been over this, m'lady. You aren't taking anything away from them that is rightfully theirs. And from what I could grasp from what your gentleman has been saying, you are planning to give them more than your husband ever intended. So to my way of thinking, you're giving to them not taking away."

Finally Eve was able to find a smile within herself and plastered it on her face. "Thank you, Gladys. I wouldn't have been able to get through these last couple of days without you. Promise you'll stay with me for at least the next year."

"Oh m'lady, I shan't leave you ever."

Eve smiled over the other woman's fervent and heartfelt exclamation but didn't allow it to touch her deeply. Life had taught her that these sorts of promises couldn't be kept. Eve was certain her mother would have made her such a promise. And Gerald certainly had. But both had left her suddenly, without warning, without preparation.

Except Gerald had made preparations. He might not have intended for them to ever be used. Eve would like to think he would have treated her differently if he had ever thought she might actually inherit his wealth and holdings.

He surely would have prepared her for it if he had ever believed it possible. Or he might have made other arrangements altogether.

That thought brought Evie up short. She couldn't be lamenting Gerald's early demise. He hadn't done it intentionally. And he might have never meant to leave her such an extensive inheritance. But there they were.

She was about to become a very wealthy and possibly powerful woman. And she had Gerald to thank for it.

She ought to be grateful. She *was* grateful. But was it morbid to be grateful for her husband's death?

Perhaps rather she ought to think she was grateful that he had made more provisions for her than she had realized and leave it at that. The man was dead. The past was dead with him. She had the future to look forward to. And she now had the means and opportunity to make that future how she saw fit.

Evangeline wished she could discuss it with Sean. He would likely have some sort of equation for her to think about, she thought with a smile.

"I'm relieved to see you looking a little lighter, m'lady," Gladys commented as she ushered Eve from the room.

"Lighter?" Eve asked with a small laugh.

"Less burdened, perhaps," Gladys explained, making Eve nod.

Her companion was right. She had been burdened. Or rather she had allowed herself to be burdened. But she was trying to throw off the lowering thoughts that weren't going to benefit anyone.

The facts were that Gerald had left his properties to her. It was odd that he had never told her about it or readied her to actually take over his affairs. Eve suspected he had considered himself invincible so heirs were unnecessary. But the fact remained that he had named her as his heir. And she had the documentation to prove it. Or her lawyer did. So she would make arrangements for the other Robertsons and then get on with her life.

A life that she was determined would be full. Full of what, she hadn't yet decided. But seeing the frequent gestures toward her midsection that Lucy kept making and the growing niggle of jealousy that continued to cause, Eve was starting to suspect she was going to want children of her own.

Perhaps she could adopt. Her face widened into a smile as she contemplated that thought and wondered if she ought to ask Sean what he thought.

Thinking of Sean brought her up short. Why would she want to discuss the prospect of adopting children with her mathematician? Why was she allowing him to hold such sway over her thoughts and feelings? She hadn't gone and allowed herself to fall in love, had she?

Eve was again glad she had chosen not to eat very much that morning as the wayward thoughts were stirring up more discomfort in her midsection. She would worry about that later. She had a lawyer to consult with.

The ride to the solicitor's office was filled with nervous chatter. Lucy seemed more nervous than usual and Eve began to worry about her friend.

"Is everything well, Lucy? If you aren't up to this errand, you should return to the house," Eve said to her quietly as they stepped down from the carriage on the busy street.

"And miss this excitement? I would never be so craven," Lucy insisted. "But I do thank you for your kind concern."

"Are you certain?"

"Absolutely," Lucy replied with a firm nod. "Now, don't give me another thought. I have jitters in my mind but they are nothing for you to worry yourself about at all. I wouldn't want to be anywhere other than here at this moment, I promise you."

Squeezing Eve's arm, Lucy gave a small squeal. "I've never helped someone set themselves up in business before. I ought to be scandalized but instead I begin to think perhaps we ought to take over the entire city."

Eve shook her head and joined her friend in laughter. "Let's start with a couple of enterprises first and see how we do."

She was relieved to see that Lucy wasn't ill, but Eve was reminded that she wasn't the other woman's only project. Curiosity and a strange bit of envy swept through her before she shook her head and followed Roderick's gesture toward the front door. She shouldn't keep anyone waiting needlessly.

"No need to hurry," Sean whispered to her as she passed by him, making Eve wonder if he could read her mind. "Remember, you are in the lead now."

A frisson of excitement thrilled through her, but Eve managed to keep her head and carry on through the door being held open for them with just a small nod in acknowledgement of Sean's words. She would allow them to warm her heart and stimulate her imagination later. For now, even if she were in charge, she had too many gaps in her knowledge to be able to lead well.

"And so you see, while I don't think you ought to feel obligated to make such a generous settlement upon the Robertsons, they have already agreed to your terms."

It felt to Eve as though less than five minutes had passed and yet an entire lifetime might have gone by. Her entire life was different. The Robertsons had accepted without a fight? She could hardly believe it.

"We have dispatched runners to guard your most valuable holdings while the Robertsons vacate them, as it cannot be guaranteed they won't cause some sort of sabotage."

Eve could feel herself turn pale at the lawyer's next words. It was an odd, light-headed sensation. She didn't much care for the feeling.

She tried not to alert anyone to her distress, but Sean must have noticed as he put one of his large, warm hands briefly on her shoulder without a word, lending her some of his strength. It dispelled the chill that had suffused her and she was able to nod and follow along as the lawyers and clerks shifted papers and continued providing more information.

"We have taken the liberty of hiring at least one new clerk at each of your offices. You don't have to keep them on beyond the initial setup if you don't wish. But since you have your economics expert to consult, we thought it best if there was at least one person in each office that you could trust would not be partial. Instead, we can guarantee their loyalty. That way, you will be able to ensure the records haven't been tampered with and can ascertain the true state of affairs."

Eve nodded along with what the man was saying but then thought of a major concern.

"Do you think it possible they have stripped the businesses of their value?"

"It is possible. It doesn't seem they were competent to any extent. But with the speed at which we were able to get in and take over, we can be nearly certain they weren't able to do any damage in retaliation. It is merely a possibility that they were trying to cover up their incompetence for the sake of ongoing business."

"So do you think I am gaining worthless enterprises?" Eve swallowed the lump of disappointment that was trying to form in her throat.

"They are currently far from worthless even if your brother-in-law lowered their value. How they carry on will depend much on you and any decisions you make going forward."

He said it in a kindly tone, but Eve could hear his skepticism. She straightened her spine even more than it already was and looked him in the eye.

"I will look forward to learning all that is necessary to make them thrive," she said firmly even as she noted the glint of approval this brought to the austere man's gaze.

"Our firm will be honored to advise you as we can, my lady," he said, finally seeming to warm to her more than previously.

"And you'll have all of our support as well, Evie," Lucy finally broke her silence as Eve clasped her hand.

"I'm still rather stunned that it has all come about so quickly."

"Hard to believe you thought you were a dependent little more than a fortnight ago," Lucy agreed with a laugh as she gained her feet. "Shall we celebrate with ices at Gunther's?"

This brought a round of relieved laughter from their party and with firm handshakes and promises of future meetings, they all took their leave of the solicitors and made their way from his offices.

Chapter Twenty-Three

Sean couldn't avoid acknowledging the swirl of disquiet that was mixing uncomfortably with the dessert in his stomach. Had it been too easy? Would the Robertsons really leave Evangeline alone?

It was hard to believe after they had taken everything from her and then had still expected her to wed for their convenience. Sean was certain there would be trouble from that lot.

But he wasn't going to ruin the festivities with his concerns.

"Would you be willing to walk back with me?" Eve asked him quietly when they were taking their leave of the fine establishment.

"It would be my pleasure," he answered automatically, hoping how much he actually meant those words wasn't too evident in his tone. After a round of handshakes and farewells, Roderick handed Lucy up into the carriage, leaving Eve and Sean on the sidewalk.

He couldn't gauge her expression as she watched the carriage pulling away. But then she sighed and turned to him and her troubled gaze was much easier to read.

"I didn't want to upset Lucy, but surely it can't be over that quickly. Do you honestly believe the Robertsons are just going to quietly withdraw from the operations they considered their own these past two years?"

Sean wasn't sure how to answer. On the one hand, he wanted to be encouraging, but on the other, she was saying exactly what he had been thinking himself.

His hesitation made her laugh. "You are thinking the exact same thing but don't want to admit it, aren't you?" she demanded without heat. Sean shrugged and smiled sheepishly.

"I was hoping to be positive," he excused.

"Well I'm positive we need to be prepared for an attack of some sort. Who knows what they might have squirreled away just in case."

"What do you mean by that?"

"It's possible they've already removed lists of clients or incriminating information or needed supplies or who knows what. This has all happened so quickly. In part to prevent that from happening, which is a good thing, of course. But it also means I have done no research or inspections of any of the properties or offices. Not that I would even know what I was looking for. I visited on occasion when Gerald was alive, but I haven't been since, so there is no way for me to say what Ralph and his sons might have changed in the meantime."

"We will help you. You know that."

"I do," Eve acknowledged with a small smile. "And I am truly grateful. But I don't think that takes away the risk or potential of Ralph, or Sabina, or even their sons, doing something that will hurt me either financially or personally. They were in control of everything at one point. I can't even say what they might be capable of doing to me."

Sean was tempted to pull her into the shelter of his arms, but they were on a busy street in Mayfair. The last thing the poor woman needed was more gossip to overcome. Surely her family was about to cause her enough trouble to contend with. But he had to actually grip his hands into fists to prevent the urge.

Eve misunderstood the gesture. With a laugh and a shake of her head she declined a potential offer of violence. "I doubt they will leap upon us from behind the hedges, Sean. I'm more concerned about some sort of sabotage at a warehouse or damage to a ship or even slander against the lending house. Any of those things could mean ruin."

"Wait and see what the other scholars might be able to do in support of you, Eve."

"Do you think a mapmaker is going to be of much help? Or an anatomist?" She scoffed.

"The mapmaker is a frequent ship traveller. There's any manner of things he might know to check for on your boats. And the anatomist has important relatives who might be able to vouch for you in some way. I would even enlist my father if need be."

He could see her soften instantly. "Oh, no, Sean, I could never ask something like that of you."

"You didn't ask, I'm offering."

Her small hand gripped his arm where it settled in the crook of his elbow, and Sean felt as though he were a heroic knight from some childhood fable, slaying his lady's enemies. That thought bolstered him and took away the threat of nausea that had been hovering over him.

He was right. They had resources. More resources than the Robertsons, even if those fiends had stolen Evangeline's wealth.

"The lawyers have determined that much of your money is intact, safe in various banks," Sean added, almost as an afterthought.

Her sudden, bright smile was almost blinding as she squeezed his arm again and did a little skip beside him.

"And from what they could tell, there is no debt owed on the Spring Street house, either. So even if the worst happens from the Robertsons, I shan't mind at all. Well, perhaps a trifle since I have quite set my mind upon becoming a scandalous woman of business."

For the briefest moment Sean's mind flooded with all sorts of possibilities but then he suddenly called himself to account and the scholar in him kicked in. "What do you mean by scandalous?"

"Well surely there is bound to be gossip about my trying to run a shipping company and the lending house and all the other things."

She looked up at him from under her eyelashes while an impish grin pulled at the corners of her mouth.

"Did you think I was about to turn to scandalous activities of some other sort, Sean? For shame."

She paused in thought for a moment before adding. "Of course, I shall have the means to do so. And if Society is about to tar me with the brush of scandal, perhaps I ought to live up to the reputation."

Suddenly Sean laughed at the ludicrous thought. "I doubt you would find it at all comfortable."

"Tis true. But none of it is going to be comfortable, is it? Learning all the things I shall need to learn, being the subject of gossip, dealing with Ralph and Sabina's ire – they are all bound to give me nightmares."

"But you will be certain that you are in the right of it."

"Will I though, Sean? That is my fear, to be quite frank with you. What if I'm not in the right of it? I am nearly certain Gerald would have preferred someone else take over his businesses. Someone other than me or Ralph. The man truly had no respect for my intellect."

Sean patted the small hand on his arm and floundered for something to say. He uttered a silent thanks to his strong intellect when inspiration struck.

"Do you think it's possible Gerald knew you would be sufficiently connected to be able to get help if needed? Perhaps he knew you would have the wherewithal to do quite well, as we can see that you will do. Even if he didn't think you could manage yourself, which, as an aside, I will point out the man would have been a fool for thinking thusly, he must have surely known you would be able to gain assistance better than Ralph could."

The wide gaze Eve cast upon him was filled with delight and she nearly stopped all sensation in his hand from the tight grip she held on his arm.

"Oh Sean, I do think you must be right. That means, then, that he meant for me to have it. That is why he bought the Spring Street house, not to withhold it from me but to gift it to me. He might not have thought me very bright, but it is likely he considered me capable. And that's nearly as good."

Sean laughed, not exactly following her logic at the end but pleased to have brightened her spirit.

"If worse comes to worst, I could always join the Scholarly Society if I cannot find my footing as a lady of business."

Now Sean's laugh deepened to a chuckle. "Why would that be a second resort? Surely you must realize the degree of dedication involved in being a scholar."

Eve scoffed. "What dedication? Here you are wandering the town squiring a lady when you ought to be at a desk with ink-stained fingers hunched over a foolscap sheet of equations."

"And well I shall be just as soon as we gain Everleigh House. Your accounts aren't going to compute themselves, surely you realize."

The gaze she cast him then was a delightful mixture of chagrin and amusement, as though she couldn't decide if he were chastising her or jesting. Sean tried to remain enigmatic, but he couldn't prevent a smile from stretching one side of his mouth. Her delightful tinkle of laughter sounded then.

"Oh, Sean, I cannot thank you enough. I know this isn't your preference. But I wouldn't have the confidence to go forward with these affairs without knowing I could trust and rely on your assistance. I promise you, once we've gotten me settled, if you truly wish to return to the Scholarly estate, I shan't prevent you. In fact, I will sponsor you myself if you have a mind to return to academia rather than the practical application of your studies."

Sean's heart stuttered in his chest. He suddenly couldn't bear the very thought of leaving her side. Suddenly, of their own volition, his thoughts made their way out of his mouth seemingly without his control.

"Or, you could keep me on forever."

Eve laughed lightly, not recognizing the gravity of what he was saying. "That would be lovely, but you shouldn't make such a commitment when you haven't even really gotten to work yet."

Again, to his delight, there was a conveniently placed parkette exactly where he needed it, and Sean was able to pull Evie out of the flow of fashionable traffic into a modicum of privacy.

"I'm serious, my lady. Would you consider taking on a half Scottish, completely illegitimate mathematician as your partner, not just your accounts manager?"

"Sean Smythe, I refuse to allow you to thus disparage yourself. You are perfectly wonderful and fully acceptable and what your parents did to you was the unacceptable thing, nothing a child ought to be punished for."

Sean could see she still didn't understand what he was trying to express to her, so he grasped her upper arms, pulling her toward himself in order to lower his lips to cover hers while she was still talking, as though she were trying to fill the space between them with her words. He suspected it was sheer bravado on her part since she didn't push him away or in any way protest his actions.

He had no wish to bring scandal down upon her, though, so despite his personal desire to stand with her in his arms for the rest of the day, he reluctantly lifted his head and stared down into her widened eyes and kiss-roughened lips.

"What was that for?" she asked even as colour flooded her cheeks with embarrassment.

"You were talking nonsense," he explained. Rather than offending her, she laughed and nodded.

"It was an effective means of making me quiet. But really, Sean, what was that for?"

"I was trying to ask you to marry me, and you couldn't seem to understand that."

The silence that followed was almost deafening. It was fortunate for Sean that he had been a student his entire life, though.

Watching his lady helped him not to lose heart.

Chapter Twenty-Four

M*arriage?*

He wanted to marry her?

Was it the money?

No, of course not, this was Sean Smythe.

While Eve was certain Sean didn't despise money, he wasn't like everyone else who nearly worshipped the commodity.

But then why would he want to marry her?

Mortification spread through her as a grin widened on his face, and she realized she must have spoken that question allowed.

"Because you are the darlingest woman to ever exist, and I find myself quite in love with you."

Eve blinked in stunned silence and the smile slid off Sean's face.

"You either loathe the idea or I've shocked you into silence, which is it?"

He asked the question so gently that Evie wanted to lay her head on his shoulder and burst into tears.

"You can't be in love with me," was what finally came out of her mouth.

Why wasn't Gladys there? How had she managed to find herself alone with the perfect man for her? If only she wasn't terrified of the thought of marrying anyone.

"It's really quite easy to do," Sean said, the laughter in his voice making Eve wish she could smile, but she feared she would never smile again.

Eve shook her head.

"It's not the right time, I know, and I'm sorry. I didn't actually intend to tell you anything about this right now. It just popped out of my mouth without asking my leave."

Finally she was able to dredge up a smile at his ridiculous words.

"But Sean, I cannot possibly wed. What about my businesses? I've only just gained them."

"I know, my darling, and I would never interfere with them."

"No, but they would be yours if we were to wed."

Eve could see understanding dawn on Sean's rugged features even as he flushed as though she had slapped him.

"I see," Sean said with a stiff nod. "Of course, that would be of considerable consideration for someone in your shoes. Since you've just regained possession of a fortune you hadn't realized had been stolen from you, I suppose it is only natural that you would suspect everyone would treat you thusly."

"Oh no, Sean, don't starch up on me now. I know you would never steal from me. But that is what happens when a woman weds."

Eve struggled to explain herself. As a widow, she could own property outright. As a married woman, everything becomes the possession of her husband. She wasn't even really that fearful of that part of marriage.

She trusted Sean wouldn't rob her. It was just the irrevocability of it. She hadn't been happy in her first marriage. She couldn't count on another husband dying so conveniently to free her if she wasn't happy a second time. Despite the morbidity of her thought or perhaps because of it, she finally found a smile with herself.

"Do you truly wish to wed with me, Sean? I thought you were far too intelligent for one such as me."

For the briefest moment, Eve thought Sean was going to kiss her again, and she thrilled to her bones over the prospect. But he held onto his control and composure and kept his hands and lips to himself, to her disappointment.

"I would expect any man who met you would wish to do so, Evangeline. You are beautiful, kind, and far more intelligent than you give yourself credit for."

Delight swept through her at his words and she tried not to preen like a cat. Instead, she blinked and stared at him.

"Do you honestly believe that?"

"Yes," Sean answered immediately. "Which part are you questioning?"

Eve knew her smile appeared slightly maniacal but she lifted a helpless shoulder. "All of it, really."

Thankfully this prompted Sean's ready laughter and he reached out a gentle hand toward her chin. Evie wasn't sure what he had intended by the gesture, but to her it was almost unbearably meaningful.

As though he were supporting all the weight in her head. The racing thoughts, the worries, and concerns. It was the most appealing impulse anyone had ever enacted toward her. And she finally admitted she had given him her heart.

"What if it's dangerous?"

Sean somehow seemed to be able to follow the convoluted way her mind worked and knew what she was asking.

But just to be sure, he asked, "Our marrying, you mean? Why would it be dangerous? Or rather, do you think our marrying would make your situation more dangerous?"

Evie shook her head. "Not more dangerous for me. But the situation isn't currently dangerous for you at all, I wouldn't think. If you're just a scholarly gentleman helping me with the maths, no one will pursue you."

"But they're going to pursue you, aren't they? The Robertsons would be your heirs if something were to happen to you, wouldn't they?"

It was as though it hadn't occurred to him.

"It's a rather large sum of wealth, Sean. I'm surprised they haven't come for me already."

"Well then, all the more so you ought to marry me. I can keep you safe."

"I'm not sure if I can keep you safe, though, Sean." His laugh should have irritated her but it was too warm and joy-filled to possibly make her angry. "I'm serious, though. Why would you want to walk into a dangerous situation that isn't of your making?"

"It's far too late, Evie. I already walked into the dangerous situation. Meeting you was the dangerous situation. I didn't ask for it, but I'll be eternally grateful for it. You are the loveliest woman I've ever met and I'll love you until I turn up my toes at a ripe old age. We'll be resplendent with life having lived well, discovering all sorts of new and fascinating adventures with your businesses and my studies. Or you'll study and I'll do business. It doesn't matter. We'll be a pair, a team, cowriters of the paper, coworkers on the projects. But you'll have to be the one to bear the babies, I'm sorry to tell you. Other than that, I swear I'll pull my share."

If she hadn't already given him her heart before that speech she would have done it afterward. Now it was

Eve's turn to pull Sean toward her for a brief but satisfying kiss.

"Very well, I'll marry you. But we can't tell anyone until after all of this is sorted."

"Do you fear their reaction? Or that it will be a distraction?"

"You are definitely a distraction," Evie agreed with a chuckle. "But I don't want to face any more scrutiny than necessary. Just until we see what the Robertsons are going to do."

Eve knew the poor man was disappointed in her but tried his best not to show it. Not so much disappointed in her as in her decision.

He was ready to crow like a rooster that he had caught the lady. She was mixing her metaphors, but it was merely evidence of the unsettled state of her mind.

Nerves jangled everywhere from the top of her head to the tips of her toes. What if he changed his mind? What if she did? What if Ralph and Sabina sent someone after her? Who was her heir? Would killing her allow them to have everything? What would they do?

"Stop worrying," Sean said firmly but with a warm glint in his eyes as he watched her intently, the momentary disappointment a thing of the past. "You have an entire team of people on your side."

"But we don't know what we're doing yet," Eve complained.

"We will," Sean returned firmly. "Within the next few days you'll be settled into your house and you'll have visited all your new offices. We'll have worked through all the numbers and you'll be well on your way to knowing where you stand and what you're doing."

"Do you really think I'll be able to do it, Sean?" Eve could hear how fearful and tentative her voice sounded and hated the insecurity it revealed, but she couldn't help it. She needed some reassurance.

"I know you can. I have absolute certainty you will do smashingly at being a businesswoman. If there is anything you don't yet know, you will find the appropriate person to ask. And I will be by your side to help in any way I can. All the scholars will be happy to help, I'm sure."

"But what about London, Sean?"

He frowned over her seeming change of subject, confused for a brief moment before his gaze met hers and his confusion cleared. "You mean what about my feelings for England? And the possibility of running into relatives I have no wish to confront?"

Eve nodded, feeling miserable.

Why couldn't she just be happy in the moment? Why was she forcing Sean to confront all the reasons he shouldn't marry her?

From someone who had thought she never wished to marry mere moments ago, suddenly she was hoping to keep him by her side forever. But she was afraid. And so she prodded.

"You are worth the risk, my darling lady. Or perhaps you will be ostracised from Society and it shan't matter." He said the final sentence as a jest, which worked to lighten the mood as Eve gasped in mock outrage and they both laughed harder than the moment called for.

"Thank you, Sean."

"For what are you thanking me?"

"Any manner of things, really. For putting up with my nervous fidgets for the most part. But also for sticking by my side. And for saying you love me."

She was speaking in a whisper by the end. Sean had to bend down to hear what she was saying but he stepped even closer on her final words, placing his arm around her in a show of support.

"You, my future wife, will make a wonderful scholar once we get all this wealth business sorted out. Your inquiring mind will serve you well, I can promise you that."

Eve was delighted with the turn of the topic. In harmony but without a word to that effect, they resumed their walk toward Everleigh House. "What shall I study, do you think?"

"I would think maths, but I suppose you'll have plenty of that at home. Perhaps you will choose anatomy or botany. Have you not thought of anything you'd like to study?"

Eve laughed. "I will be studying you for the foreseeable future."

"But of course, a noble pursuit, to be sure."

They were in fine humor when they reached the steps of the Northcotts' lovely townhouse, too caught up in their light-hearted conversation to notice that Eve's nephews were awaiting them on the sidewalk.

"There you are, you hussy. We've been waiting for you. Never thought to see you strolling along on the arm of some lowlife." Clifton spat on the ground to demonstrate his disgust.

"Shouldn't be surprised, considering she has managed to rob us of what should have been ours. It's only to be expected that she would be in such low company," Richard bellowed in reply to his brother.

Eve stiffened and was filled with a brief urge to offer violence to the two rough young men.

Sean patted her hand and stepped toward her nephews.

"We haven't been introduced. My name is Sean Smythe. Who might you two be?"

Eve almost giggled over how thick Sean's brogue became. She wondered if it was put on for show or if it were his feelings thickening his accent.

"We know who you are. You aren't fit to be her ladyship's footman let alone walking with her hand in yours. Step away from her," snarled one of the men.

Eve stepped closer to intervene, but suddenly she was surrounded by servants and others ushering her into the house.

It was all a whirl of activity, she could barely differentiate what was happening while shouting could be heard on the street that was quickly cut short before both she and Sean were settled into a parlour with tea being served. Eve felt dishevelled and disconcerted, but she knew both were a state of mind, not that anything was actually wrong with her appearance.

"What happened?" she asked, concerned as she examined Sean for signs of a struggle. He answered her with a grin.

"Lovely young men your sister-in-law has raised," Sean said with a wry lift of his teacup in salute. "They need a better vocabulary lesson, to be sure."

One of the scholars who hadn't been in Town previously chuckled as he accepted the cup of tea from Lucy. "Luce, I know you want us all to be civilized, but do you really think tea is the answer right now?"

Lucy nodded firmly. "Tea is always the answer."

Her prim tone caused the room to erupt with laughter. It was the release needed in the moment and Eve was grateful for the swarm of people.

"What are you all doing here? And were you watching the street expecting a confrontation?"

"No, we were expecting you two. You took much longer than we had expected for you to return, so we were contemplating coming in search of you. That's when we noted the loiterers and were undecided what to do about them. And then you arrived, and you know the rest. So, what took you so long?"

Evie willed her face not to heat, but there was nothing for it. Lifting her chin, Eve refused to be ashamed of the interlude in the park. They were to wed. Surely a couple of kisses could be excused between a betrothed couple. Even if they were keeping said betrothal a secret for now.

"I was excited about a certain equation I was working on, and it took some time to explain it clearly. You know how it is when it's not quite perfected, it's difficult to explain."

"Especially when you don't have paper and pen or a blackboard handy," added one of the other gentlemen without a trace of irony in his tone.

Eve's heart swelled thinking that these people were her new family. They had chosen to stand by her side. By Sean's side, which was an even greater kindness for some of the better born in the group.

It crossed her mind to wonder what the marquis thought of his grandson's associates. But that was merely a distracting tactic. She was avoiding the real issue.

"What are we to do about the boys?"

"They are hardly boys, Eve. They were as big as the footmen and were ready to brawl like the dockworkers they are."

"That is neither here nor there at the moment, though, Roderick. What are we going to do about Clifton and Richard? It's probably obvious but I'm going to state it anyway. It's nearly certain they didn't act on their own impulse. Even if Ralph and Sabina didn't send them, they were surely acting on whatever had been discussed."

"I suspect their parents wouldn't have wanted a fight in the streets, so I agree, it isn't likely they were sent here directly. What do you think we ought to do?"

Eve sighed. She was going to have to get used to great responsibility. She couldn't fault Roderick for not telling her what to do. It was for her to decide how to respond. It was she who had faced the boys and their ire, even if the insults had been hurled at Sean. They were merely repeating things they had heard. And they felt threatened.

It was usual behaviour for bullies to threaten in return in reaction to fear. That was one of the things the scholar who was studying the mind and body connection had told her when she was at the estate. She wished he had come up to Town with the others.

But she needn't worry about her own or anyone else's psyche. She just had to stay safe. Surely with those already around her, that shouldn't be too difficult to accomplish.

Chapter Twenty-Five

It took all of Sean's considerable self control not to scandalize the group by pulling Eve into his arms once more.

He should have brawled with those rough nephews of hers when he had the chance. That would have relieved him of the excess of emotions he was dealing with that afternoon, to be sure. But it wouldn't have done Evie any good, and that really had to be his priority from now on.

At least he had the other scholars to help with the situation. It was a new sensation for him, feeling as though he could rely on others. It had always been just him and his mother against the world. Until he'd met Roderick Northcott, who had decided to befriend him years ago.

It had taken Sean overlong to accept the other man's friendship, but now Sean knew Roderick was a better friend than even a brother could be. He had witnessed first-hand that blood relations didn't necessarily guarantee you the support you needed.

But these men were his family. And they had adopted Evangeline into their fold readily. Sean's heart swelled and a little more of his resentment toward the English fell away. He was the only Scotsman present.

And they were all more loyal than he had a right to expect.

"Thank you all for coming, gentleman," Lucy stood and addressed the room, putting word to Sean's thoughts as though she had read them like a list. "While Roderick and I both have siblings we're quite fond of, we readily admit that you lot are the family of our hearts, the family of our choice, as it were. And we are ever so grateful that you have agreed to stand by one another, especially in this hour of need."

She paused briefly before grinning. "And your timing was impeccable as well."

A ripple of laughter went around the room.

"Always happy to help, of course, but what can we do? I've never been much good with fisticuffs," Pierce Darby called out with his calm voice.

Sean always found him to be the most reasonable of the bunch. It probably came with the patience needed for studying astronomy.

"Your presence over the next two or three days might be all we need. There is support and safety in numbers," Lucy said.

"So you agree that it is unsafe, then?" Eve asked quietly. "I never wanted to involve any of you in anything that could harm you."

There was a ripple of noise around the room as though they all denied her words. Finally Viscount Severn said what they were all thinking.

"We might be scientists and far more academic than the sportsmen that gad about Town, but any one of us or the lot of us, would happily stand up to anyone trying to mistreat one of our own. And that includes you now, Lady Evangeline. So don't go trying to rid yourself of us at this point."

To Sean's relief, Evangeline accepted Ellis' words with a nod and a light laugh.

"I thank you all," she said, looking around the room with a warm smile. "Unfortunately, I'm not really certain what we will need to do or what we might encounter. The solicitors are supposed to be dealing with most of it. The only possible front they have no control over is the Society one. Despite their low status, Sabina has managed to insert herself into some circles and could cause trouble there."

"This should make spending some time amongst the *ton* almost bearable, then," Darby said with his gentle laugh.

"We are invited to a ball at Yorkleigh House this evening," Lucy announced. "Any of you willing to attend are included in the invitation."

There was another ripple of noise as the various gentlemen demonstrated their thoughts on the matter, but then they each stood with a bow and expressed their willingness.

"You'll save a dance for me, won't you, Lady Evangeline?" Ellis said with a gallant bow that made Sean want to plant his fist into the face of the one he had just been grateful for moments earlier.

"Certainly," Evie replied with a smile that lit up the room but brought storm clouds to Sean's psyche.

Before he could say anything to disgrace or embarrass himself, though, Lucy had shepherded Evangeline from the room, announcing they needed to make preparations. Since they weren't promised to the ball for several hours, Sean wasn't sure what they could possibly have to do, but it was one of the mysteries he would have to accept if he thought to wed the woman.

The room quickly emptied until it was just Roderick and Sean remaining. Sean was surprised to see his friend's scowl directed his way.

"You didn't really answer my dear wife when she wondered what had taken you so long. I find it hard to believe Evie allowed you to stop along the way to explain a mathematical problem to her."

"It was a mathematical problem of sorts," Sean mumbled, embarrassed to be called out on the subject.

"I know you to be an honourable soul, but the heart is treacherous as the saying goes," Roderick said, appearing embarrassed but determined. "Be sure not to compromise my wife's friend."

"I love her," Sean said in a fervent vow.

"That may well be, but mind my words. It's an unsettled time for the lady. And she has pressures mounting upon her from all sides. The last thing she needs is censure from any quarter."

"Roddie, you know I would never–" Sean couldn't even finish the thought.

"I know you would never intentionally, but now, more than ever, she's going to be under a great deal of scrutiny. You must take care."

"I swear it." Sean again spoke as a vow.

He would never do anything to bring trouble against his lady. But the sneaking suspicion filled him that his very presence would cause her trouble.

Perhaps he ought to go visit his mum until things were more settled for the lady. He must have said his thought out loud because Roderick replied.

"I am certain you can manage to assist the lady and protect her reputation at the same time. And I suspect she has need of you and enjoys your company besides. So unless you truly believe you cannot maintain the proprieties, I think it best if you remain here."

Sean bowed in lieu of a reply. Of course he could maintain the proprieties. He had been doing so his entire life. He might have been made illegitimate, but he had never lowered himself to act accordingly.

That night, they finally faced the trouble that had been brewing. It was almost a relief. Almost, but not quite.

"Why Evangeline, how very lowering of you to be seen with this baseborn lowlife at a ball such as this."

Sabina's voice carried through the large room in a rare moment of quiet in the milling crowd. It seemed to Sean as though all eyes turned in their direction, and Evie stiffened on his arm. But to Sean's shock, her face didn't display her ire. There was actually a gentle smile on her face as she drew closer to the dreadful woman and her glowering husband

"Good evening Sabina, what a surprising pleasure to see you here. I don't think I've ever seen you at a Society event, Ralph. I should have known your bravery would ensure you weren't cowering at home in defeat."

It was clear from the expression on Sabina's face that she wasn't sure if Eve had insulted her or not. She attempted to brazen it out.

"You'll never best us, you hussy," the older woman hissed.

"I wasn't trying to," Eve replied pleasantly.

"You didn't think we'd go away so quietly, did you?"

Ralph nearly bellowed, it seemed to Sean from the way everyone had stopped what they were doing to stare, but he didn't think the man had even raised his voice. It must just be the uncultured accent he'd spoken with, or perhaps the threatening tone that underlaid his words.

"I didn't, actually," Lady E returned, still with that bland but pleasant smile pinned to her lips.

Sean could see that she had noticed a pack of footmen heading in their direction, followed closely by several of the more gentlemanly scholars.

"But I'm sure the solicitors will happily work it out to all our satisfaction. Surely here and now is not the place for this conversation."

Mr. Robertson opened his mouth to accost her, Sean was sure of it, but then he suddenly proved he wasn't as much of an imbecile as Sean had suspected. He must have noticed the burly servants encircling them and shut his mouth with a barely audible growl.

"This isn't the end of this, Evangeline," he said, low but menacing.

"I do hope you'll enjoy your evening." Without further words, Evangeline swept away from the pair, pulling Sean along beside her, allowing the footmen to escort the Robertsons from the premises and the scholarly friends to surround her and Sean.

"That was masterfully done, my lady," Sean whispered to her, concerned to feel a tremor begin in the hand that clutched his elbow. Again he glanced with concern at her face that didn't display a single ounce of the emotion he thought he felt quaking through her.

"Are you well?" he asked quietly.

"But of course." She lied straight into his face with lips that had lost their colour but were still stretched into a pleasant smile. "We cannot acknowledge any discomfort, Sean. Don't let their poison do its damage."

A quick glance around showed Sean that all eyes were still upon them, and indecision was clearly written upon several faces, as though they were trying to decide if they would put stock in the Robertsons' words or Evangeline's.

Suddenly, the others were clamouring for their attention. Ellis pulled Sean away from Evie while a young woman he didn't know approached her. Sean wanted to dig in his heels and stay by her side, but Ellis whispered urgently, "Let her be for now. The speculation will die down again in a moment if you aren't by her side."

"But no one is ever going to accept me by her side."

"They will," Ellis vowed. "Just you wait and see. Trust the rest of us."

Chapter Twenty-Six

Evie watched helplessly as Sean disappeared into the crowd between a couple of his scholarly friends while some of the others hovered near her.

"I apologize for being so bold, my lady, but I'm a trained companion. I am very used to protecting a woman's reputation and am more proper than you could likely bear. We haven't met, but you may call me Miss Adams or Adriana, whichever you'd prefer."

Evie stared at this new woman, trying very hard not to frown. Why was she talking to her? What did she want of her? Why would a stranger be offering her assistance when even her own family never had done so?

"Lucy sent me," Adriana whispered, and everything lightened within Eve.

"Thank you, Adriana. I am uncertain about hiring a companion, but I could certainly use your company at this very moment."

"Oh yes, I wasn't interviewing for a position, my lady, just volunteering for the moment."

Despite her confused feelings, Eve found it in herself to laugh in the moment. Everything was uncomfortable and disjointed and she could barely know which way was up, but she knew with certainty that she had friends who would stand beside her come what may.

"Tell me about yourself, Adriana," Eve prompted, pinning a gentle smile upon herself and turning her attention away from the ugly scene she had just experienced.

"Oh, I'm dreadfully boring, I'm afraid, but I am well-versed in Society proprieties. That is my strongest suit that I can recommend at the moment. Unfortunately, while that is of benefit, it is also what contributes to my dreadful boringness."

Eve found a giggle threatening. It might be part hysteria, but she knew it was also part delight in finding a new friend who was dreadfully realistic about herself. Eve could relate. She cast fascinated eyes upon the other woman.

"I think anyone who can boast of enjoying the proprieties is far from boring."

"Oh dear, no, I didn't say I enjoy them, merely that I'm well versed."

Eve swallowed the giggle but knew her smile was stretching well beyond gentle. "Very well, Miss Adams, shall we stroll? I find myself in need of a glass of punch."

With a nod the other woman matched Evie's pace exactly.

"You are quite good at your task, aren't you?" Eve marvelled. Making the other woman, who had appeared rather mousy before, glow for the beat of a couple of steps.

"Thank you, my lady, that is kind of you to say."

"Did you actually train for the role?" Evie was curious.

"In a manner of speaking," Adriana said with a sigh. "I have essentially been a paid companion since childhood."

"That sounds slightly precarious to my way of thinking," Evangeline said, earning her an appreciative nod from the woman by her side.

"It is good of you to notice. Most just think I was fortunate to have found genteel employment when it was most needed."

Eve's tender heart, the one she had been trying so hard to keep behind barriers, didn't have its usual protections now that she had discovered love, and it nearly broke for the woman by her side.

"That doesn't sound the least bit comfortable," she said. "I admire your fortitude. You must present yourself to me at Everleigh House if you find that you are, in fact, in need of a new position. I have found that I am newly interested in having friends. And I've discovered that friends stand by and assist their friends."

Eve had never witnessed another human glowing before. It was both disconcerting and rather lovely. She was looking forward to learning how to be an even better friend in the future. But she knew she had the very best to learn from.

Lucy Northcott and her band of scholars had taught her so much, not just about science. Despite the trials she still had to overcome, she knew she had a rosy prospect to look forward to.

But she had an uncomfortable ball to endure first. It was clear that those in attendance were divided in their opinions. Half were more welcoming than she had ever experienced, the other half were turning a shoulder when she approached.

"I do hope your prospects are not diminished by your gesture this evening, Miss Adams," Eve said in a low voice after they had sipped their punch and returned to the ballroom.

"Not at all," Adriana returned, not seeming perturbed in the least.

"Might I have the pleasure of the next dance?"

Eve was startled by the invitation coming from Harlow, Sean's dreadful cousin. She thought to refuse and glanced frantically at Adriana. With an almost imperceptible wink and a slight gesture, the other woman seemed to indicate to Eve that she ought to accept.

But was it a betrayal of Sean?

That was the thought she couldn't get out of her mind, even as Harlow swept her into the steps of the waltz – a dance she had only shared once with Sean. What if he saw her?

"You are thinking too much, my dear," Harlow said, startling her out of her whirling thoughts. "It's just one dance. And I am well connected. Sean will swallow his feelings for the greater good, I promise."

"You don't actually know him, though, my lord," Eve pointed out, even though she suspected he was right.

"I know the man well enough. I know his sense of justice is very acute. And while he might not care for me, I'm certain he won't tar you with the same brush."

"Why did you ask me to dance, then? Was it to twit him, even if he will forgive the infraction?"

"Not in the least. It was in the hopes of bridging the gulf between us."

"How do you think to do that?"

"It is evident to anyone with eyes in their head that Sean cares deeply for you. Therefore, I am helping you. Knowing Sean's sense of justice, he will be forced to look at me with a little more favour after I do you a good turn."

Eve had to laugh. "So I am merely a means to an end, then?"

"I mean you no offence, my lady," the roguish man nearly sputtered as he realized he had likely offered an insult. Eve laughed again.

"I shan't take offence. I appreciate your honesty. It isn't the most common trait."

"Especially not in these environs," the viscount agreed readily.

Eve looked at him with greater interest, intrigued despite her reluctance.

"So one of your parents is a sibling to Sean's father?" she probed.

Eve knew she ought to know, but since she had never made a proper debut, she had never bothered to memorize the book that all debutantes swore by to know who was who amongst the *ton*.

"Yes, my mother is Sean's aunt."

"Do either of them acknowledge the relationship, then?" Eve enquired, fairly certain of the response.

"Not in the least, although, that is more for lack of opportunity on my mother's side. Sean has, up until now, avoided Society as though it carried a dread disease. It was only last Season that he came up for the first time with his friend, the youngest Northcott boy."

Eve laughed anew. The viscount with whom she danced couldn't be much older than Roderick was, if at all. Harlow flushed but didn't retract his words, meeting her gaze as though daring her to comment on them.

"That boy is doing a great deal of good for your cousin and the other gentlemen scholars who might make great, life-changing discoveries. You shouldn't disparage his efforts."

"I wasn't disparaging, my lady. Is he not the youngest Northcott?"

"I believe he is, but he would likely argue he's a man, not a boy."

Harlow shrugged and Eve shook her head. She couldn't decide if he were amusing or annoying. Knowing Sean didn't much care for this part of his family made Eve lean toward annoying, but she suspected the roguish man might just be trying to be brazen. Or perhaps he was actually trying to be helpful and just had an odd way of going about it. He had invited her to dance when she was feeling awkward after Sabina's attack.

Throughout the night, it seemed to Eve as though she were the most popular she had ever been. She was handed from earl to viscount to marquis to baron with a few opportunistic fortune hunters to liven up the partnering.

She only caught glimpses of Sean through the crowds and only managed a very brief greeting in passing, but he seemed to be similarly occupied, except that his partners were all well placed matrons, which amused her to no end.

Evie looked forward to hearing his thoughts on the matter on the morrow. It was likely the work of Lucy, but he was sure to have feelings on the topic.

The next morning, over coffee in the breakfast room, Eve was surprised to find most of the household present and clamoring for attention.

"You danced all night," Lucy complimented as she filled her plate and took a seat next to Evangeline. "I am surprised to see you up already."

"I'm even more surprised to see you up and about, don't you have need of extra sleep these days?"

Lucy grinned. "Don't be a nursemaid, Evie, it doesn't suit you."

Before Eve could think of a comeback for that statement, Lucy had turned the topic to Sean. "What did you think of Society's leading ladies, Mr. Smythe?"

The jest was evident in both her tone, her dancing gaze, and her use of the formal address. Sean barked a laugh, much to Eve's relief.

"It's only fortunate that Severn had already caused me to realize my painting an entire nation with the same colour as my father was an oversimplification," Sean said, stunning everyone into silence. The silence didn't last long, though, with Lucy present.

"Whatever did Ellis do to cause such a turnabout?"

Sean shrugged and appeared embarrassed to have said anything.

"He was my friend," Sean finally said, causing a ripple of laughter around the table. "Prior to that, I thought Roderick was an aberration. Seeing that Ellis could be human, as well, gave me cause to start rethinking my hypothesis."

This prompted more laughter and good-natured teasing amongst the men.

"But you were right," Sean said, recovering his composure and interrupting the hubbub that had followed. "The matrons have the best understanding of things. And if you can charm them, you're set."

"Did you manage to do so?" Lucy asked appraising him like a schoolmaster.

"But of course, did you ever doubt it?"

"Not in the least," Lucy answered immediately. She again turned the subject. "I know it's last minute, but I do hope you will all make yourselves available. My sister-in-law will be hosting a ball tomorrow night and would like you all to attend. If any interesting announcements need to be made, they could be done there, with her blessing."

Eve was startled by Lucy's significant glances, as though she ought to know what the woman was talking about. Did Lucy think she ought to announce her inheritance? Would that not be a remarkably low-class thing to do?

The *ton* was always appreciative of spending money and loved gossiping about any who had an excessive amount of it, but one never acknowledged it if one had been so blessed.

Then her gaze enmeshed with Sean's and she felt heat tinge her cheekbones. Did Lucy mean their betrothal? Had Sean told her?

She didn't think she was ready, but she also didn't think Sean would spread tales. Perhaps they were merely more transparent than she would like to think. With a sigh, Eve knew she had work she needed to do before she could be settled.

She was about to push back from the table and leave the room when Roderick surprised her by saying, "When you have some time, this morning, Eve, my father and I would like to meet with you to discuss a few matters."

Flutters of nerves sprang to life in her midsection and Eve was relieved she hadn't eaten much.

"I am at your disposal," she said with a nod. "When would be most convenient for his lordship?"

Roderick's smile was one of approval. "Shall we say in about thirty minutes? He is likely nearly ready to entertain company."

Eve was surprised but relieved that she wouldn't have to agonize over the question of what the earl wanted to discuss with her. Perhaps they thought her presence too disruptive to the household and she ought to remove herself. That was fine.

It was even just as well, as long as the lawyers had secured the Spring Street house. And surely that was basically a sure thing, as long as Ralph and Sabina didn't sabotage it somehow, but Eve didn't think they even knew about that house, as it had never been mentioned in her hearing. Unless they thought to keep it a secret and then gift it to one of their sons if he were to wed.

Eve's thoughts were in such a whirl that she was nearly a frazzled mess by the time she reached Lord

Everleigh's library. She paused outside the door and wiped her nervous palms down the front of her gown.

She was born into the nobility, she reminded herself. There wasn't anything for her to be intimidated about in this nobleman's presence. And with how kind Roderick had been to her, surely he must have found that kindness from somewhere. Perhaps the old earl would be pleasant to deal with.

"Come in, don't hover," came the gruff command, and Eve's hopes shrank until she met Roderick's smirking face when she stepped into the room.

"Introduce us, my boy," the earl commanded, amusing Eve after she had just defended against the use of the word *boy* in connection with Roderick Northcott.

Eve dipped into a deep curtsy as she accepted the invitation to the Earl of Everleigh.

"You have livened up our dull existence, Lady Evangeline." The earl surprised her by smiling as he said it. "I have been nearly agog to meet the young lady to whom Robertson left his considerable wealth. I'm only sorry no one realized it ought to have been you sooner. It's almost certain his incompetent brother has lessened your coffers considerably in the time since the poor fellow passed."

Eve blinked. She had not been expecting this when she was called to meet the earl. She wasn't sure what to say in response. But the earl didn't seem to be expecting one, as he carried on.

"Have you had an accounting yet? Are you going to come about or could you use some assistance? My son Adelaide is always looking for interesting ventures to invest in, should you have need of an influx of the blunt."

Heat burned through Eve's chest, but she recognized that while a touch of it might be polite discomfort with talk of money or business, most of it was the unusual experience of having someone offer her assistance.

While Lucy and Roderick and their scholars had already been lovely toward her and she was growing comfortable with their interference, she was uncomfortably aware that it had started from Lucy's strange sense of obligation toward her.

Lord Everleigh had no such reason. He was merely being kind. It was a novel experience.

Eve lifted her chin and dipped another curtsy. "I thank you, my lord. That is the kindest offer I have ever received. And you show me what I can aspire to with my new circumstances."

She wasn't being flattering, she knew as resolve spread through her. "I hope I shan't need the assistance, but I will draw comfort from knowing there is someone who could offer it if I find that I am mistaken."

The earl surprised her with a bark of laughter.

"You'll do, my lady," he said with a nod of approval. "Now come and indulge in a bit of lowly business talk. I would like to know what you have planned."

Eve's gaze flew toward Roderick, who only lifted a negligent shoulder and gestured her toward one of the chairs in front of his father's desk.

"Would you prefer privacy?" Roderick asked after settling her in the chair.

"If you are interested in staying, I am certain you would have some valuable insights to add," Eve said. "In fact, once things have settled into place for me, I might be interested in investing in some of the gentlemen's inventions or ventures, so it would be good for us to see if our thoughts align."

"This one has an independent streak three miles wide, Lady Evangeline. It isn't likely he will allow you to stick your paddle in his little boat."

Eve smiled gently. “Perhaps he might be more interested in the assistance of someone who isn’t his father or one of his older brothers.”

The earl’s eyebrows nearly met his receding hairline and he shouted another bark of laughter.

“She has your mark already, doesn’t she, Roddie boy?”

With that, they settled into a surprisingly intelligent and informative conversation that Eve found both educational and comforting. She wasn’t surprised to find the earl so intelligent, just that he appeared comfortable discussing things she thought most nobles left to their stewards and solicitors. But by the end of the hour, she found he was informed and involved in similar dealings as she would be embarking upon.

In fact, he was one of her business partners in certain of Gerald’s ventures. It made Eve feel protected in an odd sort of way.

The rest of the day passed in a blur of frequently changed gowns, received calls, a visit to the solicitor to sign some more documents, passing brief conversations in low tones with Sean that sent thrills through her, and then finally, with a sigh of relief, Eve settled into a comfortable seat at the theatre, prepared to be entertained.

Of course, she had forgotten that the *ton* considered much of the entertainment to be staring at and gossiping about each other rather than paying attention to what was happening on the stage, so Eve found the sound of conversation that swelled around her irritatingly distracting until the music and pageantry on the stage finally sucked her in and allowed her to disappear for an enjoyable interlude. In the back of her mind, she was aware of Sean’s comforting presence at her side, but he didn’t intrude on her enjoyment, perhaps merely enhancing it as she felt cared for despite her lack of attention.

When the curtain dropped and the conversation was interrupted by half-hearted applause, Eve had to blink herself back to reality but felt refreshed from the brief reprieve from the hectic situation her life had become. The Everleigh box was full to nearly bursting, but Eve appreciated the display of support.

She was well aware that several of the gentlemen would much rather be anywhere but at the theatre. Their relief at the conclusion was palpable and they were delighted when Roderick offered to take them out to some rougher establishments after they returned the ladies to Everleigh House.

Sean's concern for her lead him to offer to remain at the house with her, but Eve assured him she would be retiring for the night so if he wished to carouse with his friends, he wasn't to feel tied to her apron strings. Eve wasn't sure if his grin was over her terminology or anticipation of a night of sowing wild oats with his friends but she was far too fatigued to be troubled over the matter.

When it felt as though she had barely settled her head on the pillow, suddenly the room was flooded with sunlight and Gladys was whispering that she had Eve's morning chocolate if she wished to begin her preparations for the day.

"How is it possibly morning already, Gladys?" Eve asked with a plaintive note to her voice.

"Despite being a lady, me thinks you aren't used to the ways of the *ton*, m'lady. And besides all the running around sorting out your business. But surely it should all soon be arranged and you can settle into as quiet a life as you'd like."

"But not too quiet, I hope," Eve agreed with a grin around the rim of her cup. "I do look forward to having a choice. While I'm sure I shan't be the highest *ton* once it becomes known that I've gone into business, it doesn't seem as though I shall be cut from Society entirely either."

"Not if Mrs. Lucy has any say over the matter, in any case," Gladys agreed. "But that Mrs. Robertson seems to be trying her best to make it so."

Eve sighed.

"Sabina is not accepting reality graciously, I'm afraid," she agreed. "But Mr. Brown has been able to get Ralph to sign agreement to everything. They will take over Gerald's house as well as accept a financial settlement. Mr. Brown was a shrewd negotiator. I had been willing to offer even more than Ralph accepted, but Mr. Brown started the negotiations much lower and they agreed well below what I had thought was bearable. Mr. Brown thinks Ralph and Sabina will end up selling the house and setting themselves up in something smaller and more affordable, which makes much more sense to me, but I know Sabina was hoping to save face. The good news is, I shall be able to retain the servants I'd most like to bring with me to the new house. It isn't large or grand, so I shan't need a full staff like Gerald's house required. We shall soon be perfectly comfortable."

"Are you not comfortable here, m'lady?" Gladys asked as she shook out the gown she planned to dress her mistress in shortly.

"Oh, perfectly comfortable, but this isn't my home. I truly wish to have a home of my own. That's what triggered this entire venture in the first place. It has turned a trifle more complicated than I had expected, but the house I'll be moving into is exactly what I'd like."

"Are you really going to take over running all those businesses, m'lady?"

Eve frowned over the worry she could hear in Gladys' voice and stared at her intently for a moment.

“What is the concern? Do you fear for my reputation? Or worry it will make too much work for you?”

“Oh, no, neither of those. Now that I’ve grown to know you better, I know you’re too much of a lady to allow your reputation to be damaged. But I do worry a little for your safety. And I think you would delight in having children.”

Eve stared for a moment.

“Well,” she began before pausing in thought briefly. “Businessmen have children all the time, so I don’t see how I couldn’t do so if I so wished.”

“But will you?”

Eve sighed. “For one thing, Gladys, I wasn’t so blessed before, when I did nothing but sit around and be ornamental. It’s entirely possible I cannot do so.”

“Oh no, m’lady, forgive me for bringing up what must be a painful subject then.”

“No, no, don’t trouble yourself. I haven’t gotten to the point of fretting about it yet. And Sean assured me that one of the scholars is studying anatomy and might be able to assist if it turned out to be an actual problem.”

Gladys appeared scandalized. “You’ve discussed such a matter with him?”

Eve laughed. “He did ask me to marry him, I thought it only seemly.”

Gladys sputtered a little more but couldn’t argue with Evie’s logic. Eve carried on.

“The thing is, if I wed Mr. Smythe, he will help me with the businesses, so it seems that if we were so blessed, I would be in a position to do both business and motherhood if I so wish.”

“That sounds wonderful, m’lady, and again I apologize if I’ve overstepped.”

Eve accepted the servant’s offer of assistance from the bed and allowed her to begin the process of styling her hair for the day. After a space of silence Eve met her maid's gaze in the mirror.

"You made yourself my first friend, Gladys. You are allowed to express your concerns to me. I will try to be reasonable and listen to them. They are valid. But I had already considered most of it. Now I just need to get through the remaining few complications and we can almost hope for a fairy-tale ending to this story."

"Whatever do you mean?" Gladys asked, laughter sounding in her voice.

"Don't the best stories end with living happily ever after?"

"Surely yours shall, m'lady."

"Only if Sabina and Ralph can be kept from turning into the ghouls who ruin everything."

They certainly tried.

The rest of Eve's day followed a similar pattern to the day before. She was able to access the house she planned to move into and saw that it had been well kept and was ready for occupancy. The servants she had opted to keep from Gerald's house were already readying their new place for her to move in. She only had to make a couple of adjustments and buy a bit more furniture for it to be completely habitable.

"Perhaps we could choose together," she murmured to Sean when he helped her into the carriage behind Lucy to return to Everleigh House to prepare for that evening's ball. The grin that stretched his face felt like balm to her nerves as she faced one more large Society event before she could settle into her new life.

"Thank you for inviting me," Eve said politely as she was introduced to their hostess, Lucy's brother's wife, Viscountess Simmons.

"We are always happy to help any friends of our dear Lucy," Lady Isabelle said, causing a slight wrinkle of confusion to mar Eve's forehead.

As they made their way into the ballroom, Eve tried not to appear as though she were hissing as she asked Lucy, "What did you do?"

Lucy's attempts to appear innocent were unsuccessful so she pulled Eve into a small alcove behind a potted plant.

"Don't be angry," Lucy implored.

"I shan't be angry if you tell me what is happening. I also might need to be told why you didn't think to include me in the planning of whatever you have arranged."

"Oh, Evie, don't be irritated, we thought it for the best, I swear it to you."

"Of course you did because you can't help but feel it your right to arrange everyone's lives for them," Eve began, anger splashing through her. But she quickly reined that in. It was one of Lucy's loveliest charms. At least when it didn't put Eve in an uncomfortable position.

"Never mind, I'm sorry, I shouldn't be angry. I know you do these things from the best of intentions. But hurry and tell me. Roderick will be looking for you in about a minute and a half."

Lucy grinned over that last sentence, which had been Eve's intention. She really couldn't hold a grudge against the interfering woman. Lucy clapped her hands, delighted with herself for her own machinations.

"Ellis has arranged for everyone to be here. Even if Sabina turns up again somehow, you will be flanked by all the highest members of the *ton*. The marquis might even bring Prinny with him."

Eve stared, unable to comprehend Lucy's words.

"I beg your pardon? What does Viscount Severn and, I'm assuming you refer to his grandfather when you reference the marquis, have to do with your sister-in-law hosting a ball this evening?"

"Oh, Belle thought it a delightful challenge. She was thrilled to see how quickly she could pull together a crush and whether or not guests would appear. And look at it. She will be overjoyed with the evening's success."

"Let me understand correctly. You had your sister-in-law plan a ball in order to make sure I appear well ensconced in Society?"

Lucy nodded happily.

"What if it had fallen flat? A last-minute ball means everyone had already accepted other invitations," Eve pointed out, watching intently as Lucy's face brightened further rather than falling as she had expected.

"That's where Ellis comes in. He arranged for all the gentlemen to call in their connections. Thus Prinny's possible presence. The marquis, you know that's Pierce's grandfather, almost never goes to balls, so his promise to appear will make it impossible for anyone to refuse the invitation. And Jasper, I don't know if you've met him yet, but his father is the Marquess of Wheaton. He's the one who's friends with the Regent. From what I understand, it was almost easier to get His Highness to consider coming than to convince the marquess. But in the end, everyone was excited at the opportunity."

Eve stared at Lucy a moment longer, trying to decide if she were pleased or mortified by this development.

"What about Sean's connections?" she asked quietly. "How uncomfortable is he likely to be tonight?"

"We didn't go so far as to invite his father, but Sean agreed that we ought to invite Harlow and Harlow's mother. Sean is feeling ready to embrace certain English elements, if you'll recall from this morning's conversation," Lucy concluded in a prim tone that finally brought Eve to laughter.

She pulled her friend into a quick, unfashionable display of affection, hugging the woman tight before stepping back and straightening her fichu.

"You are the best honorary sister a woman could hope for," Eve told her, grinning as Lucy's eyes filled with tears.

"Oh, you beast, you know I'm completely emotional these days. I always wished for a sister."

Evangeline laughed. "You have adopted me into your family of scholars. I don't claim to be one of those, but I will happily support the Scholarly Society in any way I can."

"I know," Lucy said, linking her arm into Eve's elbow and pulling her back into the crowded ballroom. "Roddie told me you will be a benefactress if we need one."

Eve grinned. "His father wasn't sure if he ought to be pleased."

Lucy nodded but then turned serious. "Oh dear. Sabina just entered on the arm of that dreadful baron she seems so enamored with."

"Not Baron Heath?" Eve said. "Is he still in Town? I thought he was returning to his estate after seeing to his banking."

"Be on your guard, my dear friend," Lucy whispered. "If he is a client of your lending house, she might be trying to stir up business and social trouble at the same time."

"I think you've provided enough insurance," Eve countered with a smile as Viscount Severn approached with a dignified older gentleman in his wake.

Eve pulled herself up to her full height before dipping into a deep curtsy as she was introduced to the Marquess of Wheaton. She couldn't help marvelling at how much her life had changed in only a few weeks.

The evening was a smashing success. Lady Isabelle had filled her ballroom with the matrons Sean had sweet talked the night before as well as all the noble family members who, though they tried to lament their relative's insistence on science, couldn't help but be proud of them and support them in any way they could, even if it meant accepting a lady business owner.

A short while later, Eve watched with a mixture of delight and dismay as Baron Heath loosened Sabina's grip on his arm and then strode toward her, leaving the older woman in his wake as footmen began accumulating around her.

"My lady, I do hope my presence here hasn't caused you discomfort," Heath said as he bowed over her hand formally.

"Not at all," Eve replied, glossing over the truth in favour of *politesse*. "But I must inform you that I don't hold with discussing business at balls."

"No, of course not," the baron said approvingly, assuring Eve that she was correct in that regard at least. "But I will whisper to you that I will continue to keep my business where it currently is. It would seem I will be in good company."

Eve allowed her gaze to drift around the room. She wasn't certain all the wellborn relatives of her scholarly friends would be able to countenance doing business with a woman, but she was glad the baron didn't need to know that.

She had no intention of relying on her acquaintances to keep her businesses afloat. But she would accept the support they were willing to lend her on the Society front, at least.

Despite Sabina's efforts to cause trouble, it didn't seem Eve was going to be shunned. But Eve knew she would have to deal with the Robertsons anyway.

She politely took her leave of the baron and made her way to the side of the room where Sabina was in the center of a knot of scholars and footmen who were steering her out of the ballroom.

Despite her determination to cause trouble, Sabina couldn't help seeing she was defeated at least for the time being.

"It seems you have won all, Evangeline," Sabina said in a cold, angry tone that she managed to keep low enough not to cause a bigger scene.

"It didn't have to turn out quite like this," Eve began.

"Of course it did," Sabina scoffed. "Gerald should never have left his will in such a way. It should have been Ralph's, and well you know it."

"Gerald didn't agree with you. But I have never wished ill for any of you. I do hope you can find your way to being happy, Sabina."

Sabina sniffed and turned her head away, giving Eve the cut direct. Despite her discomfort, Eve couldn't help being amused over the other woman's determination not to accept the inevitable. It was shocking to her that Ralph was seemingly more reasonable. Eve had truly believed Sabina had meant her well during the time they had shared a home. That had clearly been a ruse.

"You didn't like her anyway," Sean said, surprising her by suddenly appearing at her side and seemingly reading her mind. "It's doubtful you could have successfully become friends, so don't let it trouble you. She will find her footing now that she has accepted the reality. Everyone will make sure of it."

Eve turned her attention to the gentleman by her side. "I am marvelling at your about face, Sean. Thank you for all of this."

"I had little to do with it, to be honest. I can't believe Severn went to such lengths."

Eve smiled, her heart warming anew. "It would seem we have a wonderful family."

Sean smiled into her eyes. "That we do. Would you allow me to announce it now, then?"

Eve's eyes widened. "Do you mean our betrothal? You think to announce it here? Won't that steal some of Lady Simmons' glory?"

"Surely you jest," Sean scoffed. "It will be the finishing touch on her night if she can have a last-minute crush and a scandalous betrothal to boast about."

"But there's nothing scandalous about it," Eve argued with a giggle. "The Scholars have seen to that."

"Exactly," Sean said. "Let's just add a bit of spice to it." And with that he lowered his head to drop the briefest kiss onto her surprise-parted lips.

It was just enough to cause a ripple of excitement to flow through the room as the orchestra brought the cotillion to an end and Sean tapped his glass to gain even more attention and prevent the next number from beginning.

"Everyone, I would like to ask that you join in our joy. Lady Evangeline has agreed to take me on. Please, congratulate me. I am to wed."

Eve joined in the round of laughter that filled the room. It wasn't the most romantic declaration, Sean had already done that privately. But it was perfect to gain the support of all in the room.

They were almost crushed by the surge of support that came their way, and Eve had to fight against tears of joy as she knew her fairy-tale was about to come true.

Epilogue

Ellis, Viscount Severn, watched his friend's announcement with a slightly jaundiced eye. It was possible he was jealous of the other man, but Ellis Dorval didn't want to admit such a lowly thing of himself. He ought to be happy for him. And proud of himself for the assistance he had offered his friend.

And of course, he was both of those things. He had done a good thing. It hadn't been that hard to convince the other scholars to scramble together as many of their High Society relatives as possible to attend Lady Simmons' ball. Well, it had been a challenge to tear them away from Lady Evangeline's treasure hunt, to be sure, but they had all promised Lucy they would support the ball, so it hadn't been too much of a stretch to get them to bring a relative.

Even Ellis' uncle, the Earl of Beaverbrook had deigned to attend. Of course, that fine gentleman was in search of his next countess, so he could always be counted on to attend Society functions. The more the better in his estimation. Whatever it took to replace Ellis in the succession.

It was one more reason why Ellis was envious of Sean's discovery of happiness. What a feat for the mathematician. He found endless math problems and true love all in one fell swoop. No wonder Ellis was jealous. He could lose his uncle's patronage and lineage all at the drop of an infant if Beaverbrook were to successfully sire a son.

Now was not the time to be thinking about it, Severn reminded himself sternly as he accepted a glass from the tray of the passing footman. He tossed back the wine in tribute to his friends' happiness. He was happy for them. Truly.

He would just have to find his own source of security and happiness next.

The End

Intrigued by Ellis' interference
and the companion's intervention?
And what about the treasure hunt?

Enjoy the next read:

A Chemist and A Companion

When handsome scientists and High Society collide, chemistry is sure to follow...

New to the Northcott world? Want to see where the Scholarly Society started out?

Read about Roderick, his brothers, and their friends in the *Northcott Kinship* series.

An introductory novella:

Assisting Lord Richmond

She'll *never* love him. Not again, anyway...

Book One:

Intriguing Lord Adelaide

She's a wallflower debutante—and his best friend's sister.
But one dance could change everything.

About the Author

Wendy May Andrews learned to read when she was four or five, listening to her mother read when she was lonely, feeling separated from her brother after he started school. Ever since, Wendy has had her head buried in books. She loves words – historical plaques, signs, even the cereal boxes – but her first love has always been novels.

Many years ago, her husband dared Wendy to write a book instead of always reading them. At first, she didn't think she'd be able to do it, but shortly after starting her project, Wendy realized that she loves writing. Those early efforts eventually became her first published book – *Tempting the Earl* (originally published by Avalon Books in 2010). She said: "It has been a thrilling adventure as I learned to navigate the world of publishing."

In her conversations, Wendy is often heard saying: "I believe firmly that everyone deserves a happily ever after. I want my readers to be able to escape from the everyday for a little while and feel upbeat and refreshed when they get to the end of my books."

When not reading or writing, Wendy May Andrews can be found traipsing around her neighbourhood or travelling the world with her favourite companion.

Stay in touch:

Website Facebook Instagram TikTok

Stay in touch with Wendy May Andrews
and all her upcoming publishing news

Sign up for her biweekly newsletter at
wendymayandrews.com

Other books by Wendy May Andrews

See the entire collection!

Scan the QR code below

Made in the USA
Middletown, DE
20 March 2025

73018507R00150